Liz Crowe Earns 5 Stars for Stewart Realty Series

"Banter and absolute need for one another when they were together was positively combustible, and it had me switching from angry to aroused every other minute! The BDSM elements are light but sensual, woven in seamlessly yet not pushed on the reader in any way. Beyond the main Sara and Jack story line, I loved the secondary characters in Floor Time, and I'm hoping that book two in *Stewart Realty* series, Sweat Equity, features more of Sara's brother Blake and his partner Rob."

~ Just Erotic Romance Reviews

"It's raw, emotional, strong, confusing (to them at least), heart-wrenching and completely FANTASTIC! Their love & sex burn the pages and make me want that fabulous ending, since their road has been so tough, I have to know the rest of their journey and what the future holds for them."

~ Hesperia Loves Books

"Her characters are interesting and likeable and their interactions are realistic. Jack and Sara are each the epitome of the successful, driven and self-absorbed salesperson. Their mutual attraction makes (a lot of) risqué sex easy for them but they must both work hard to learn to trust and how to make their relationship work. The secondary characters are well written and add to the story. Crowe's descriptions of the life of an active REALTOR are spot on although I've never had the kind of fun selling houses that her characters do!"

~ My Book Addiction Reviews

"A sexy, thrilling ride of passion and real estate. When Jack and Sara come together, they combust. It doesn't matter where they are or who is around them, they can't keep their hands off each other. As they explore their cravings, they experiment with a little BDSM and Dom/sub [interactions] during their love making. The scene at the open house will leave you breathless."

~ Sizzling Hot Reviews

" Floor Time features characters that must learn about what they want, need, and just how to go about getting it. Jack and Sara are in the same work field, and they instantly draw sparks when they meet. Jack has a past that he'd rather keep hidden despite urging desires, and Sara is independent, fierce, and stubborn. Liz Crowe creates believable characters, a fast-paced plot, and oh my, the sizzling love scenes. This is an erotic and satisfying read with all the elements of a good book rolled into one. If you're a fan of contemporary erotic romances, love series, and a story with a hot male lead and feisty female lead, don't miss Floor Time!"

~ Storm Goddess Book Reviews & More

"Love that both characters are strong, smart and flawed. Jack is the hot alpha male that all the women want. Sarah is the smart, sexy woman trying to work hard to get ahead in the cut throat world of high priced realty. Can he really commit to one woman? Can she let herself trust him and allow them to have a relationship? Great writing, hot sex, and well fleshed-out secondary characters."

~ The Review Studio

"Liz Crowe has introduced us to the fast-pace and high-stakes of real estate with Floor Time. The ups and downs of real life are the hallmarks of this book, accented with great sex scenes and relatable characters that come off the pages and into your life. Ms. Crowe scores a home run with the Stewart Realty series."

~ Book Babes & Coffee Faves

Other Liz Crowe Books
From Sizzlin' Books:

Stewart Realty Series:
Floor Time
Sweat Equity
Closing Costs
Essence of Time

Standalone Titles:
Vegas Miracle

Coming Soon:
Escalation Clause (Stewart Realty Book 5)

You can find out more about Liz Crowe and her
books (including a complete backlist)
on her website: www.lizcrowe.com

Sizzlin' Books is a Division of Tri Destiny Publishing
Find us online at www.sizzlinbooks.com

Liz Crowe

Floor Time

Sizzlin' Books
A Division of Tri Destiny Publishing

Floor Time (Stewart Realty Book 1)

A *Sizzlin' Book* published by permission of the author

Printing History
Sizzlin' Books Edition January , 2012

Copyright © 2012 by Liz Crowe
Cover Art and Design by JJ Silver Designs

ISBN: 978-0-9569669-7-1
Sizzlin'Books are published by Tri Destiny Publishing

Printed in the United States of America

PROLOGUE

Sara put her palms against the ice-cold glass of the floor-to-ceiling windows. She smiled, observing the entire downtown of Ann Arbor spread out below her like a child's carpet map. The heat rose visibly from the pavement as the crowds scurried in and out of restaurants and shops.

Adam's arms around her waist startled her. As she turned, a niggling voice at the back of her brain made her hesitate before brushing his lips with hers. They'd been in the vacant condo way too long. Now that he'd teased a satisfactory orgasm from her neglected body, an antsy, nervous sensation wormed through her psyche. She sighed and disentangled herself from his embrace.

The doorbell echoed through the cavernous space, making her break out in a cold sweat. Fumbling with blouse buttons, she pushed past Adam on her way through the kitchen and to the door, cursing under her breath. She looked back to make sure he was pulled together – not a tough thing since neither of them got completely out of their clothes – and scowled as he gave her a knowing smile.

Shit. You should not have done this. You don't even really like him. But it had been so long and he was pretty good looking. Jesus, slut much Sara?

Sara let guilty thoughts clang around her head long enough to hear the doorbell ring once more before yanking it open, her perfect pleased-to-see-you sales smile fixed in place, keys clutched in one hand.

Jack had a hot date, one that was going to yield him a kick-ass listing, but due to the unwarranted dawdling of the condo-shopping couple he had been dragging around, he'd be lucky to make it in time. The empty lock box on the door of the penthouse unit provided the real icing on the cake. He leaned on the doorbell, hoping they could skip this one and stop wasting his time while mouthing platitudes to his clients. He had hoped that the relocating, executive couple like the ones he was courting at that moment wouldn't spend so much of his valuable time arguing over granite colors and the relative benefits of central vacuum cleaners. God, he hated this job sometimes. He smiled, and turned, hearing the click of the deadbolt. Finally.

When the heavy door swung open, the vision standing there froze him mid-sentence. Sara Thornton, one of the newer, and more successful, agents at Stewart Realty, stared at him, eyes blazing in a strange combination of aggravation and satisfaction. Jack clenched his jaw at the sight of her smoking hot body encased in skintight short black skirt, creamy silk blouse and four-inch stilettos.

As one of the few chosen to populate the downtown storefront office, based upon her good looks and the ability to rope in new buyers and sellers off the streets of Ann Arbor, Sara had serious sales skills. He'd studied the branch's numbers, as part of a management decision-making process, ultimately turning down the offer to handle that stable of prima donnas. But at that moment Jack couldn't believe he'd never noticed her before – *really* noticed her. Where had she been hiding? And what was that amazing sexy aura that permeated the air? Jack's heart jumped in his chest.

"Um, hi Jack," her voice was hoarse, making him blink. He made a conscious effort to wipe the idiotic look off his face, aware of the annoying clients still standing at his elbow. He held out a hand, needing to confirm that her skin felt as hot as it looked. Surprised no one else saw the sparks pass between them, he couldn't suppress a grin at the look on her flustered face.

So, she sensed it too. This could get interesting.

"Sara," he heard his own voice, sounding a hell of a lot more confident than he felt at that moment. And he did not rattle easily. "Sorry to barge in but…" Once again he was dumb struck by the sight of Adam Donovan, mortgage broker tool, at Sara's shoulder. Jack gave himself a mental shake. The sudden realization of what had undoubtedly happened, in the same condo he was about to show, made his head pound. Reluctant admiration mixed with something resembling jealousy fogged his brain. He raised his eyebrows at the tall blond man whom he could have sworn was engaged to someone else.

"Jack." Adam moved around the beautiful woman who still blocked the doorway. "Good to see you."

Jack shook the guy's hand, never taking his gaze from Sara, reserving his smile for her. His brain clicked into focus, locked on Sara Thornton, and the world shifted under his expensively clad feet.

Sara had never been more embarrassed. No, that was too weak of a word – mortified was better. Jack Gordon, king of the Ann Arbor real estate universe wanted to show the condo where she'd just let Adam Donovan mercy fuck her. As she tried not to drown in Jack's deep blue gaze, Sara clenched her thighs, already imagining how he might have done it differently, and likely better.

"Um, hi Jack," she croaked out. Her face flooded with heat; even more so when she put the keys in his outstretched hand, and yanked herself back at the intensity of their instant connection. Tall, ruggedly handsome with coal-black hair and a shimmering blue gaze, the man boasted a personality that bested all other males within a fifty-mile radius. Sara only knew of him, of course. They'd never actually met. However, she'd swear right then he seemed happy to see her. The realization made her zing from scalp to toes.

She watched his full lips form words but remained deafened by the roaring in her ears. His gaze never left hers, even when Adam nudged her aside and shook his hand. Her whole universe suddenly shrank to two people. Looking back, she'd pinpoint that as the instant she fell hopelessly in love with an impossible man.

CHAPTER ONE

Sara sat straight up in the bed; the sheet wrapped around and between her legs, the alarm jangling in her ear. She ran her hand through her sweaty hair and attempted to calm her pounding heart. She came to grips with the fact that she had been dreaming about Jack Gordon – again – then realized she had come in her sleep.

Again.

Damn.

Her mind skipped through the long list of tasks she had to get through that day. She glanced at the clock – five a.m.; an ungodly hour, but the only time she could fit in a run. Sighing, she flopped back onto her pile of pillows and closed her eyes, foregoing the run and hoping for one more hour of blessed oblivion, before tackling the hectic workday ahead. She had a couple of deals on the ragged edge of falling apart, plus new buyers to mentor, and a few sellers to hand-hold; not to mention a huge transaction that she held together with a glue stick and the sheer force of her will.

How could she have known she'd encounter Ann Arbor's most successful realtor and most eligible bachelor on the same day she'd finally shaken off her losing streak with guys and apparently scored with Adam? Jack's mischievous grin and deep blue eyes as he had appraised her frazzled, post-orgasmic self, had left her speechless that day and haunted her days and nights ever since.

Showered and dressed by nine, Sara headed out the door on her way to the office when her phone buzzed. A mystery number, but she took the call anyway, as any decent realtor would.

"Sara Thornton," she grabbed her laptop, mind half on the to-do list already.

"Hey, Sara, it's Jack," the deep voice that had invaded her dreams that morning seared her nerve endings. Sara's hand tingled where he'd touched her handing over the condo keys.

"Oh, um, hey there. What's up?" Laptop forgotten, she slumped against the wall, hearing herself babble.

"I just wanted to tell you about a house I listed."

Sara tried to calm her breathing and let him fill the silence that ensued.

"Yeah, I got it signed up yesterday, actually. It's in your neck of the woods, where you do a lot of business."

"Where? I mean, I've got listings sort of all over right now." She swore at herself for sounding like a stupid rookie.

"I know, but you tend to list in the Lansdowne area a lot, right? I've got a great deal there – kids listing mom's house since she's moved over to the retirement village."

"Um, sure, well, I grew up there so everybody pretty much knows me." Sara's sales hackles rose at the thought that someone had taken a listing out from under her. She had just that week met a woman who was considering listing her mom's house – a striking tall blond, who had seemed ready to sign with Sara but had "one more agent to meet first." Sara realized who that "one more" must have been. Her face flushed with anger, no longer aware of Jack as a desirable man, but as a client-stealing asshole. She stomped to her car, jerked open the door and tossed her stuff into the back.

"Yeah, my uh, client said she knew you, but I guess she liked me better," he chuckled.

"Well, whatever. Are you calling to gloat or actually tell me about the house?" In a flash of disturbing erotic images, Sara realized that the stupid blond had likely demanded a piece of Jack's fine tail in exchange for it. She gripped the steering wheel, took a deep breath and waited for him to speak.

"Oh, it's one of the tri-levels, a piece of shit really, grandma's décor and the whole ten yards. But hey, it's Lansdowne, right?" Sara sucked in a breath. *Bastard knew how to turn the knife didn't he?*

"Yeah, okay, how much," she ground her teeth. "And you'd better give me a number somewhere north of three hundred."

"Oh really," he teased, perhaps not realizing she was serious. "And why is that, pray tell Ms. Thornton."

"Because, you jerk, 'it's Lansdowne' and I have some credibility there, telling people value all the time." Realizing she'd called him a jerk, she groaned to herself.

Nice one, Sara, way to impress.

Jack laughed and it sent another spark shooting from the top of her head through her entire body.

"Seriously, I know, I know. I'm just fucking with you."

"Whatever, Jack, I'm busy. Don't you have better things to do than call me up and throw the fact you stole a listing in my territory up in my face?" She pulled into the parking lot behind the downtown building that held her office, got out, retrieved her briefcase, and slammed the car door. "Well?" she shouted into the quiet phone.

"Relax babe, it's all good – these people are gonna be a pain the ass, I can tell so consider it a gift from me to you."

Sara's face burned, as she recalled last night's dream, and acknowledged what sort of gift she'd really like to get from him. She shook her head at herself.

"Gee, thanks, *hon*. Do me a favor and spare me at Christmas? I can't imagine what you'd consider an appropriate gift then. Take care now, bye-bye." She hung up before he could respond. Sara stood and stared at her phone, completely amazed at herself. Christ, she'd just hung up on Jack-fucking-Gordon – the goddamned master of the Ann Arbor real estate universe and recent star of her most explicit sex fantasies.

Stomping into her the storefront-style real estate office, Sara took deep breaths and poured a cup of much-needed coffee. Served the asshole right, really, she shrugged and sipped on her way to the front of the office. But his voice still echoed in her ears.

Jack grinned and put his arms behind his head. The blonde woman – his new client, he reminded himself – emerged from his bathroom, dripping from a shower. Suddenly, he badly wanted it to be Sara standing there with a well-fucked look on her face. The woman before him had an alarmingly predatory look in her eyes. He sat up and made his way towards the bathroom. He had an eleven o'clock closing and needed a shower. She gripped his bicep as he passed.

"That was fun Jack," her voice, so sultry and appealing in days past grated on his nerves now. He reached down to remove the hand she'd wrapped around his cock. Talking to Sara on the phone, imagining her smile, those eyes, had made him rock hard. He tried to find the words appropriate for the "thanks for the fuck, now leave" moment he was about to have. His nearly visceral need to feel Sara's body under his practiced hands was making him insane. But he had resisted, being a real gentleman about it, if he said so himself. Staying back a bit, just observing her and asking around. The time had come, time to make his move.

"Yeah, baby it was. But I gotta get going." In typical fashion, his body took over, and he let it lead. "Oh, well, if you insist." He pressed her up against the door-jamb and swept his tongue into her mouth. As she wrapped herself around him, Jack shut down the part of his brain that was starting to remind him he was nearly forty, unmarried and unattached, and a little bored with his current lifestyle.

After the near-miss marital fiasco he'd endured out of law school, he'd made a solemn vow: fuck first, questions later. It had worked fairly well. He'd built a reputation, made his first million five years ago without a family to support, and had a virtual black book most men would give their left nut to possess.

He sighed and picked the woman up, dropped her onto his bed and proceeded to bring her to screeching orgasm with his lips and tongue before donning a condom and plowing into her body. He shut his eyes at the last moment, as his climax roared up from the base of spine and hit his brain. He hoped he didn't call out Sara's name because hers was the face he saw beneath him as he came.

CHAPTER TWO

Sara didn't even look up, intent on her mission to the fax machine while reading an email on her phone, as she rounded the corner of the front sales desk. A sure grip on her arms kept her from plowing straight into a firm wall of strong, blue-suited torso planted smack in the middle of the front office. When she lifted her eyes they met Jack's. The look he shot her – a little curious, somewhat questioning, very intense – brought tingles to her scalp. To her knowledge, he'd never even darkened the door of the downtown office before today.

Could he sense she was having sex dreams about him? Did he read her like a damn book even though they weren't that close, merely fellow realtors at the same company? He had used his amazing charisma and stark, Black-Irish good looks to their full effect through the years. He was a millionaire twice over thanks to them, but had never entered into her small orbit until now. His reputation preceded him, and Sara's mind reeled with tales of female conquests in real estate offices, empty houses and various semi-public places.

"Whoa, hang on! Don't go so fast. You're gonna hurt somebody," he laughed. Sparks flew from his touch straight to her core. His eyes widened; then narrowed, as if sensing her reaction. She made a show of jerking her arm out of his clutches.

"Hey, sell that Lansdowne house yet, big boy?" she threw over her shoulder, eager to get some distance between them before she embarrassed herself. Summoning every ounce of willpower at her disposal, she endeavored not to stare at him, open-mouthed, as he leaned against the counter in his dark blue suit, French-cuffed shirt and perfectly matched tie. Her brain did its little song and dance routine again reminding her that he was bad – very bad – and her own apparent, unfounded obsession with him had to stop.

"Hell no, and you know it."

"So why are you here, if not to aggravate me?" She pretended to fight with the fax machine. Anything but meet his eyes again.

The sales secretary appeared at her side in a flash. Sara frowned at the simpering look on the young woman's face as she stared at the man-vision before her.

"Hey Jack."

Somehow, Sara knew he had fucked her. The girl was practically lying on the counter to get his attention. Of course, he was a sight worth seeing, his windblown, thick hair practically begging for her fingers.

"What?" He dragged his eyes from Sara. "Oh, hey babe, how are ya?"

Incredible. He doesn't even remember her name. Sara, avoid this guy like the plague.

Sara's sales manager chose that moment to emerge from her office. "Jack, to what do we owe this distinct and, no doubt, well-planned honor?" Pam crossed her arms in front of her ample chest, looking pointedly over at Sara then back at him.

"Pamela, good to see you too." Jack faced her, one elbow still leaning on the counter. "I was just down the street in a meeting with architects. We're doing that kick-ass renovation over on Washington – mixed-use – retail and condos. Should be done in about a year or so." He trailed off and looked straight back at Sara.

Sara couldn't concentrate – which pissed her off. She was not about to fall into the guy's trap. She was well aware of his rep. She had neither excuse nor reason to be infatuated with him.

Anyway, she needed to focus on Adam's closing and the recent hitch in their whirlwind relationship.

Screw Jack.

Oh yeah. Bad choice of words.

She breezed by him heading back to her desk.

"Bye," he hollered at her retreating form. "Tell Adam I said 'hey'."

That last comment made her turn to look at him. He had one eyebrow raised, still leaning on the counter – a damn advertisement for manly perfection – absolutely the worst possible thing for her. Sara ground her teeth, turned back around, and raised her hand in a mock salute good-bye.

Jack eased himself into the late-afternoon downtown Ann Arbor traffic. The near perfect waning summer day made him crank his car windows down, and the satellite radio up. He had money in the bank, a woman in his bed and frustration rustling around in his brain. He cursed whatever weak compulsion had led him into Sara's office. The strange impulses he'd fought for weeks since encountering her at that condo were annoying. He'd done everything he could to quell his need to see her, to touch her, again.

The blond client had provided some distraction from his alarmingly intense obsession with Sara but had proven to be a real handful lately. She wanted his constant attention, sent him texts all day long, and had seemingly taken a vow to drain every ounce of his sexual energy. He always thought that well was pretty deep, but her clinginess had gotten real old, real quick. A couple of times she'd even pleaded with him to forgo the condom. The second time she'd asked, he'd cut the scene short, furious with her for even asking again. He'd bolted from her place that night, his gut aching with something more than simple unrequited lust.

The phone buzzed insistently on the seat next to him. He sighed. *Back to work.* But his thoughts kept drifting in a Sara Thornton direction. This infatuation or whatever he had buzzing around in his brain was going to kill him if he didn't do something soon. Her perfume ghosted through his senses. Jack repressed a groan of frustration as he pressed the phone icon on the steering wheel, prepared to handle whatever shit storm had developed in the last half of his day. He idly wondered if she realized she was dating a man engaged to be married and made a mental note to stay on top of how that unfolded. She might need a shoulder, and he planned to position himself correctly when the need arose.

Sara dressed in her best suit the morning of Adam's closing. His purchase had been smooth – a real anomaly in today's real estate market. As a mortgage broker himself, the loan portion had been seamless. Despite her pique at his recent disappearing act, Sara looked forward to seeing him and making up with a bottle of wine and cooler of cheese and fruit in his new expensive space.

What had started as a hot hook-up in the very condo Adam was closing on had led to an intense three-week period of dates, intimate dinners, and flowers delivered to her office – the very sort of thing that many nearing-thirty-year-old women would have given a Manolo allowance to have. Sara had loved it, had given in briefly to fantasies of big weddings and suburban McMansions. Her natural tendencies to avoid emotional connection, thanks to her parents' volatile relationship, had been hard to overcome but, she'd been trying.

The fact that Jack-fucking-Gordon, the client stealer, had inserted himself into her dreams and fantasies hadn't helped one bit, however. Sara had caught herself more than once picturing his bright blue gaze over hers, imagining his large hands on her flesh, all while she was supposed to be making love with Adam. Staring at herself intently in the hallway mirror of her small condo, Sara attempted to ignore the little voice that kept reminding her that Adam honestly was not so great in bed but, he'd made up for it with his wildly romantic gestures – at least until recently.

She shrugged off the looming doomsday sensations. *Beggars can't be choosers. Adam is a great guy, who would make a very lovely, stable spouse and would no doubt coach little league and do all the shit your own dad never did.*

Sara took a deep breath and tried to get her mind to pinpoint what was truly bugging her as she threw the car into reverse and mentally ran through the reasons she had to avoid a man like Jack and hold onto one like Adam. The conversation she'd initiated with one of the agents who'd known him nearly ten years ran through her brain on a repeat loop.

"Jack Gordon? What d' you want to know? How many millions he's made or how many women he's fucked?"

The man could not possibly be interested in her. No way. Enough to randomly stop by her office? Ridiculous.

The gossip she now got on a regular basis backed up his rep as a cocky, womanizing jerk and then some. The mature, good girl in her felt he was best left to the likes of her secretary or wide-eyed vacuous clients, like the one he'd stolen from her. Sara knew she was strong enough to resist Jack, but something about him made her want to see him, to be around him, and that compulsion irritated the shit out of her. The wind ruffled her hair and cleared her muddled brain. Feeling stronger and more in control every minute, she parked in the title company's lot and gave herself a little pep talk.

Adam must be reacting as many men did when they started to actually feel something more than simple lust for a woman. Yes – that had to be it. He had been trying awfully hard this week to get back in touch with her. Of course, she'd ignored him, making him work for it a little. Sara smiled to herself in anticipation of how she'd make her recent bitchy attitude up to him later.

Maybe she should settle down. Her mother, father, and brother harped on it enough. She liked Adam and wanted her family to be happy with her. However, at the same time she truly enjoyed her independence. Something in her resisted the exterior pressure to "mate" and "reproduce" even at nearly thirty. She needed something else. Something she had yet to identify, but which had hovered ever closer in the past few weeks for some reason, just out of reach.

Sara breezed into the Arbor Title office where Adam's deal was closing, greeted the receptionist and the other realtors gathered in the lobby, each of whom were waiting for their own transactions to commence, as subtle misgivings began stirring in her brain. They all looked at her a bit strangely, but she tried to brush it aside. Kim, the closing officer, ran up to her, a stack of legal documents clutched in her arms with an unusually stressed look on her normally calm face. Kim never got rattled, no matter how difficult a closing.

"Oh, hey Sara, um, your uh, client is here already."

"OK, well, let's get going then," Sara looked at her, trying to figure out what caused the unflappable woman to seem positively wigged out. "What room?" she asked, trying to get Kim to focus.

"Oh, well, down here." The woman motioned, indicating the second door.

Sara started to move in that direction, but Kim put her hand on her arm to stop her.

"Sara, you should know," she started, just as Adam walked out of the room.

"Hi Sara." He didn't move from the doorway. "I tried to call you to let you know I'd moved the time up an hour – I had a last-minute conflict so…"

Sara stared at him, realized what he was saying – her closing had happened without her there. She started to walk towards him on autopilot.

"Oh, well, gee Adam, I could have used this hour for something else I guess."

He moved toward her, and she had the distinct feeling he wanted to head her off, to keep her from entering the closing room. Her temper flared as she walked past him, eluding the hand he held out. Inside the doorway, Sara took in the sight of a perfectly gorgeous young woman seated at the large table. She looked up at Sara and smiled.

"Oh, hello, you must be Sara." The woman had a charming city-bred English accent. She stood and stuck out her hand. "Adam has told me so much about you. Thanks for your help with all of this. I've been away a month getting my mum sorted out; she's been ill so…" The woman kept her hand out, waiting for Sara to take it.

Sara stayed frozen to the spot but recovered enough to touch the woman's palm. She blinked stupidly while her brain focused on an enormous diamond ring on her left hand. The room darkened, and Sara had to remind herself to take a breath. Kim grabbed her hand and slid a chair under her collapsing body.

"I'm Lou – Louise, actually, but no one calls me that. I'm so looking forward to getting all settled here. I'll be at the U, finishing my residency." She babbled on, completely unaware that Sara nearly passed out from shock as the vision of what she had been doing with this woman's fiancé for the past month ran, montage style, through her head.

Adam stood outside the door, one hand on the jamb, the other on his waist, his head bowed, as if praying. Lou gathered her stuff and walked past Sara to join him. Kim held out a cup of water. Sara suddenly realized why the other realtors in the lobby had been staring at her. The reality of the whole mess nearly suffocated her. Kim turned to face Adam and his fiancée.

"Well, ok, then, thanks guys and congratulations." Sara watched her glare at Adam who wouldn't meet her eyes. Lou stuck her hand out again since Kim didn't seem inclined to do so first.

"No, thank you, and you too Sara," she leaned around Kim who blocked Sara from view.

Sara stood up realizing what she had to do. She fixed her professional smile in place and shook Lou's hand before reaching out for Adam's. She stared at him – her own face neutral while her brain spun its endless loop of that first encounter, when she'd gone against everything rational, let go of her long-developed reserve, and let this man fuck her silly in an empty condo.

Livid, mortified, and facing the hard reality that once again she'd managed to fuck up her own love life in front of this entire goddamned office, she watched them walk out the door to their new life together – in the condo she'd sold him.

Kim tried to reach for her but Sara held her hand up, not willing to give in to her public defeat. She looked up at the ceiling and willed the tears back. It was her own stupid fault. She knew she should not have gotten involved with him, but she had anyway in her typical, fuck-logic-lets-have-some-fun sort of way. That's what had gotten her to where she was.

She had no one but herself to blame – although he was certainly responsible for the bit about not telling her he already had marriage plans. She sighed and walked out the door, not speaking to anyone.

A hot wind dried the tears forming in her eyes. She resolved to stop her selfish behavior, get her focus back where it belonged before Adam had interrupted her. She did not need a man. She knew that – *had* known that – but she'd let her body's need for contact overrule her brain. This would never happen again. Not even for Jack Gordon. Most especially not for him.

She sat in the car, collected herself and then drove towards her office, her mind already on the work ahead – deals to be closed, clients to be contacted, money to be made. She added Adam and the memory of today's shock and humiliation to the steaming pile of shitty love-life moments already occupied by the college boyfriend who'd dumped her on graduation day, and shoved them all to a small, dark recessed corner of her mind. She made one more resolution: Never rely on a man emotionally – get what you want if you must physically, but emotional needs were best met by friends, family and in your own head.

Once parked, she grabbed her phone and erased Adam from her contacts. *Hope he realizes he just lost one of his best referral sources. Asshole.* The tears she'd held back streamed down her face as she sat in the sweltering car.

CHAPTER THREE

Sara's phone buzzed, nearly falling off her desk before she could grab it, with an incoming text.

"295, take it or leave it. I'm dying here Sara!"

"I'll get back to you" she shot a text back before heading to her desk to call her buyer.

After nearly a year, the most difficult buyers of her career had decided that Jack's stale Lansdowne listing was their dream house. She'd been forced to deal with him almost constantly for the last two weeks. It exhausted her pretending she didn't thrill to the sound of his voice or that her scalp didn't tingle in anticipation when she caught one of his incoming texts.

After the Adam disaster, Sara had spent a solid year ignoring men, including Jack. She'd disciplined herself into a smaller skirt size, used the time to hone her career onto a serious fast track, with referrals and closings piling up along with her bank balance. Her brother, Blake, who owned a successful brew pub in town, worried about her single-minded obsession over work and her lack of any "social life," but she reminded him that the last time she had one of those, that guy had married someone else.

Sara and Blake had grown up very close. She relied on him and his partner, Rob, for most of her emotional support – and her meals. Rob was a French-trained chef, who, coincidentally enough, had been a fraternity brother of Jack's at Michigan State. He'd filled Blake's ears with tales of Jack's reputation. The coincidences and connections boggled the mind, really.

Sara sighed and dialed her buyer's number once again. She wouldn't touch Jack Gordon with anyone's ten-foot pole. The fact that he had stayed out of her way fairly effectively hadn't escaped her notice.

Figures. He probably senses you're kryptonite.

And now this. She had buyers, who seemed to get off on Extreme Negotiation; and his seller didn't want to close any deal. Mainly because it meant she wouldn't get any more contact with her "Special Realtor."

Jesus. What a soap opera.

She shut her eyes when her buyer answered, preparing for yet another round of death by nickels and dimes. But visions of Jack Gordon's impish blue eyes and full lips swam through her mind, distracting and annoying her. Sara reminded herself once again that she was a better woman for avoiding him, for focusing on herself and her career all this time. Her body begged to differ, already reacting to the concept of having Jack in direct proximity once again.

"Ok, we finished the inspection and there are some issues, as you might expect." Sara prepared herself for an earful.

"I don't doubt it."

Jack seemed quieter than usual, not filling the phone line with his usual *poor me, why can't you control your people* bullshit. Her suspicions grew, wondering if he was messing with her, trying to catch her off guard somehow.

"Well, um, I'll get back with you, probably tonight, with our conditions for contingency removal."

"That's fine. I'm used to getting screamed at by her anyway." A deep sigh filled Sara's ears. "Let's hold this one together, shall we," he finally asked. "I can't take much more of this seller."

"Fine, talk soon." She hung up without letting him respond.

Sara put her hands on the steering wheel before starting her car, trying to control her shakes. Why did she let him get to her anyway? Hell, he was just a guy for crying out loud. All guys were complete assholes as far as she was concerned.

Focus, Sara, focus. You've been fine since Adam, no need to fall back into this game with anyone now, much less a guy like Jack.

Jack leaned back in his chair after she hung up on him once again. He stared up at the familiar ceiling of his office, sighed, and stretched his arms over his head. His mind drifted back, as it had so many times, to the moment he'd first laid eyes on Sara Jane Thornton.

His assistant Jason stuck his head in the door, nearly making Jack dump himself backward onto the floor. His eyes sprung open erasing the image of Sara's deep green gaze – and gorgeous rear view – from his mind.

"Jack," Jason fiddled with his earpiece. "She's calling again – where are you this time?"

He groaned. "Fucking-A, why can't the woman take a hint?"

He'd had gone a lot of years able to escape serious commitment. The one time he'd allowed himself that luxury he had got bitten on the ass so hard he'd been reluctant to sit much since. The fact that the ass-biter had been his first foray into a Dom/sub relationship had made her betrayal that much worse for his ego. Now, he'd miscalculated, once again; had severely misread the blonde woman's motives.

Jason shrugged, already taking the next call. He'd been Jack's assistant for ten years and was used to his boss' love life. He'd proven himself invaluable more than once, deflecting one woman or another. Plus, he was a spot-on licensed assistant when it came to the business of real estate. Jack leaned into his keyboard, ignoring Jason again. The young man waved a hand in front of his face.

"Dude, what the hell am I supposed to tell her?"

"Tell her I joined the Peace Corps, moved to Outer Mongolia and am unavailable for the next ten years. Christ, I don't know. That's why I hired you; make some shit up."

"I'm on it," Jason turned and moved down the hallway towards his office, already making excuses.

Jason was worth his weight in salary. He'd come up with something. He always did. For about the millionth time that week, Jack wished he'd never, ever met the crazy blonde client.

But, in the most perfect of ironies, thanks to Sara, he got to deal with her daily. Jack looked back at his computer screen. Images of Sara covered the monitor – from her real estate website and blog mostly. She had a real handle on using social networking. And was a pro at keeping fresh photos and testimonials from happy clients.

Jack ran a hand through his hair. Never in his adult life had he felt so attracted to a woman who had no apparent interest in him beyond professional. Of course, he was stuck dealing with a crazed bitch of a seller he'd been trying to ditch, just so he could stay in contact with a woman who seemed determined to avoid him. An alien state of affairs for Jack – not one he liked much. His phone buzzed.

Sara.

"Yeah." He kept his voice gruff.

"Okay, I emailed you their list of stuff. It's long and pretty ridiculous though, I won't kid you."

"I'll see what I can do."

"Ok, thanks." She stopped, not hanging up for a change.

Jack felt himself relax at the sound of her voice. He smiled, pictured her eyes, her hands, her lips, and had to shift in his chair. He tried not to acknowledge the things spinning in his brain. The suddenly vivid image of Sara, naked, on the bed, wrists tied in front of her and on her knees...*whoa, what the fuck*? He rubbed his eyes and refocused.

"So," he said, as he leaned back again. "Looks like we're stuck with this deal, huh?"

"What?"

"Well, your cheapskate buyer sprung for a fairly expensive inspection. I assume that means we are on and will have to play this little game for a week or so but will ultimately consummate."

He could sense her blush through the phone.

"Yeah, he's a real pain, but sounds like you've got a similar issue on your end, eh Jack?"

"You know I do," Jack rolled his chair so he could kick the door shut. He reached over and flipped his iPod speakers on. He wanted a bit of privacy and in his frigging fishbowl of an office, he had to work to get it.

"So, I saw you running yesterday." Jack's let his tone shift into a deeper register.

"Oh, really, where?"

"Over by Pioneer," indicating the west side high school she'd attended. "You swing your arms too much you know."

"Thanks for the tip, coach."

"You look good though, generally," Jack smiled into his phone as the strains of the Rolling Stones permeated his office. "But you probably know that.

"Thanks, I think," she tried to sound nonchalant, too busy to bother with him.

Jack knew better. He knew it was time to reel this one in. Best to hang up and not chat anymore or he'd be tempted to actually ask her out, something he wasn't quite sure he wanted to do yet. The compulsion to act, yet hold back at the same time made his head pound.

"Well, I gotta run babe. I guess you've given me my marching orders. I just got your email." Jack would have gladly talked to her for the next couple of hours, but knew he couldn't sound too eager.

"All right, good luck with your seller. I'm sure you can convince her of anything though, huh?" He winced.

"Not anymore," Jack rolled his eyes as he remembered how incredible she'd been, until she lost her mind and started telling everybody they were getting married. Married? *Holy fucking shit* – he'd almost had a heart attack when that had gotten back to him in the form of a congratulations email from Greg Stewart, owner of his brokerage firm. He sincerely hoped Sara would turn out to be more reasonable. Marriage did not appear on his to-do list, not now, and not anytime soon. The sound of Sara's laughter at that moment made him sit up.

"Well, do your best or at least half as good as you *think* you are. That oughta cover it."

Jack grinned. He'd done his homework. Found a couple of younger agents in his office who had gotten up close and personal with her so he'd been able pick their brains. Their consensus had been she knew how to have fun, been easy to talk to, able to chat, flirt and generally enjoy herself. She'd send messages with her body language according to these guys, but they had both struck out, royally.

She'd kiss – very well, they both observed – touch, act like she'd be ready for third base or whatever, then completely shut down as if a switch got flipped to the off position. Neither man could move past anything but a quick grope in the car or in the front hall of her condo. Jack didn't think these were guys who gave up that easily. But she'd not gone out with either of them after the first date, and he found himself even more intrigued by her once he'd gotten this information.

He loved women – all types of women. Loved their company, their scent, the feel of their skin under his hands, and most of all he loved how he could make them feel. He prided himself on it. The potential of Sara Thornton moaning and begging for him got him revved up like nothing had in a long time. He'd become determined to be the one to release her from her apparent cycle of sexual frustration.

His body responded every time he pondered the concept of that little project. That tool, Adam Donovan, had indeed burned her a year ago. She'd withdrawn into herself, and he'd gotten busy and preoccupied, until now. Now, she invaded his dreams awake and asleep; something in her brought it out and while it titillated, it also distracted, made him short tempered and antsy.

He remembered smiling wickedly at his computer as he glanced over her buyer's original offer. It had been a shitty start, a clear indication that her buyers would be difficult. This meant their potential time together would be extensive. Jack would not only save the day, by convincing his seller to sell accept the offer, but could take his time fixing what ailed Sara. And fixing she needed. That much was clear. Whether or not she'd like his methods remained to be seen.

Of course, he'd had to concentrate on keeping the listing after he'd lost control of the blonde psycho seller. He'd had to duck a flying crystal vase at one point, but he had quick reflexes so that worked out fine – the ultimate goal had been achieved.

Jack knew timing was everything. You had to be in the right place at the right time, on purpose in order to succeed in his business. The fact that Blondie had gone *loco* on him just about the time he realized that Sara had gotten royally screwed by that broker tool had been exactly that – timing. Sara needed something she wasn't going to get with her endless routine of exercise and work. The fact that he had developed a minor obsession with her didn't escape him, but he chalked it up to lust and his usual desire to obtain the seemingly unobtainable.

Jack had lost count of the women he'd "loved." Frankly, he loved every woman he was with, while he was with them. He loved learning how to press their buttons, what made them tick, how to make them happy, or at least content, under his talented hands. But ever since law school, the one time he'd let himself really love, really opened up to a woman who'd dumped him without ceremony the very week they were graduating, he'd closed himself off to anything beyond physical satisfaction. When he sensed any emotional connection seeping in, even from him, he'd cut off the relationship, leaving many an unhappy lady behind.

He closed his laptop and headed out the door to his next appointment, feeling at the top of his game, but with a small, annoying tickle in the back of his brain whispering Sara's name.

Brushing a hand over his rough jaw, he pondered his options. He felt certain of one thing: it was time to act. He tamped down the urge to just take the direct route, scoop her up and take her to his house for a nice long weekend of bonding. No, she needed to realize what she wanted first.

CHAPTER FOUR

Still sitting at her desk on a Friday night, Sara had never felt so exhausted. She'd spent the past two weeks focused on nothing but the damn deal with Jack. He'd taken the opportunity to get all friendly with her and they'd had some long chats. He loved to text message her with thinly veiled messages about hooking up, but he never managed to ask her out on an actual date. The annoyance crossed with irritation was a buzz.

It had been an abnormally hot June. The bustling office had finally emptied. Sara had changed into comfortable clothes and faced a solid hour or more of work before heading home. She'd just pulled her hair up into a ponytail and focused on her computer – when her phone buzzed.

"Hey, Sara, I'm driving by your office right now." The sound of Jack's deep, raspy voice touched off something in her, as it did every time. Her brain slowly processed that he proposed a face-to-face encounter. *Like now.*

"Are you there? As if I didn't know?" he laughed. "I have a document for your buyer and I thought I'd just drop it off and save us some time."

Shit.

She glanced down at herself. Sara loved spending her hard-earned money on great clothes, but didn't have any of them with her tonight. She ran into the office bathroom, yanked out the ponytail holder in her hair, and tried to remember if she had lipstick in her purse.

"Sure!" she claimed brightly. "I'll meet you at the door."

She used the toothbrush she kept in the office bathroom closet, and splashed water on her flushed face. Anger at the fact she felt nearly frozen in place by the idea of Jack Gordon – that he planned to simply "stop by" after hours to see her made her dizzy. In spite of her resolve to be strong, something yearned for him, in a way that utterly terrified her.

Yeah, well fuck that. Of course he's interested in you.

She pep talked herself all the way to the front doors – a wide expanse of glass facing Ann Arbor's main street. She heard the roar of his engine before she saw the car. Sara rolled her eyes. *A Stingray. What else?*

Taking a deep breath, she steeled herself against the coming onslaught. She had work to do and would not be distracted by this – she couldn't afford to be. But her body began to betray her; her panties already damp at the thought of him in her personal space. It was a familiar feeling. She'd been having wet dreams about him for the better part of a year. She sighed, determined that he'd likely never measure up to her fantasies but realized her hands shook as she reached for the door handle.

Yeah, OK, girl, settle down. This is Jack Gordon, every woman's dream date. But he's only here with paperwork.

She shook her head, looked up and there he was – all six foot, four inch, dark hair, blue eyes, sexy white smile, of him. Resisting the sudden compulsion to look away, to not meet his eyes, she smiled back.

"Hey gorgeous," he began as he always did on the phone, his voice a low growl that matched his car engine's rumble. "I've got something for ya."

"Ha, I'll just bet you do," she threw back. *Lame*, she thought as she took in the sight of him in his dark blue suit trousers, striped dress shirt with French cuffs emphasizing what had to be an

incredible torso, arms and chest. Jack boasted a classic male shape –
wide shoulders tapering to a slim waist and long legs – and he wore
a suit better than anyone Sara had ever seen. His red and yellow tie,
which stopped just short of being loud, flung over his shoulder from
the ride. He smelled great too, some combination of spice, cigar and
leather.

Damn. I'm screwed.

"No, really. My asshole seller agrees to your asshole
buyer's requests post inspection; I've got it all signed up here. Now
all we lack is a good appraisal, and we are golden my lovely!"

"You call all the girl agents that, I'm sure." She sighed and
reached for the paper he held out, grazing his hand in the process.

His skin was warm. No, not warm, hot, as if he'd been near
a fire. She shivered unable to help it. The tingling in her scalp
crawled down her spine and settled nicely between her legs.

She drew back. He moved forward to fill the empty space
between them. Their silhouettes darkened the entry foyer. He
remained shy of touching her – keeping just out of reach.

"You know, I was looking for an excuse to see you in
person," he began. "I'm really gonna miss our little evening chats
once this deal is done."

"Yeah, well, you know where I live." Sara waved in the
general direction of the office as her breath caught in her throat. "I,
um, gotta do some, you know, busy work tonight so. . . "

Don't go...don't go... don't go.... Sara tried not to let her
face betray her inner begging.

"So do I really – but I just can't help thinking that we could
come up with something a bit, I don't know. . . more fun to do
together," his voice tempted

"Um, yeah, I guess we could go out if you want, but I'm not
really dressed for it." Sara's brain fogged over. Was he asking her
out on date? Before she could respond, react or even move, his lips
covered hers.

Her mind immediately grasped the fact that the entire
downtown of Ann Arbor could see them sucking face in the
vestibule of her office. Her manager would really not be pleased.

Oh dear Lord.

As he became more insistent, Sara responded, her psyche screaming with happy release. His lips were softer than she would have thought, but became increasingly more demanding that she share and open her mouth to him. She gave in, parted her lips, and placed her hands on his firm chest with her last bit of resistance swirling down the drain.

He licked her lips, nipped at her bottom one, and then swept inside, possessing her with his tongue. She gave way, fully aware that *this* guy, wanted by so many, held her, right there, and had reached under her hair to tug her closer. Sara had not fully acknowledged her level of own horniness until that moment – when the man who represented everything so wrong for her prepared to blow apart her world with the touch of his hands and mouth.

Jack had kept his body slightly separate from hers during their initial contact, as if he might be gauging how she would respond before committing himself. Once she opened her lips and took his tongue into her mouth, he moved closer, grasped the back of her head with one hand, his fingers twisting and threading through her hair.

Any hesitation he'd shown disappeared completely as he moved his mouth off hers. His other hand traveled the length of her back and reached up again to cup her head. He flitted over her ass, teased, seemingly determined to draw it out until she asked for more. Her traitorous arms wrapped around his neck, as she rose up on her tiptoes.

Oh my God don't do this Sara. Just. Don't.

But the compulsion that had built over the past year commanded her, and she molded her body to his as if it were the most natural thing in the world. A loud knock on the glass made her jump away and run her hand through her hair as the college kid on the other side laughed and mimed a blowjob, until his buddies drew him away.

She glanced up at Jack, saw his skin flush with anger or passion, she wasn't sure. He smirked as he watched the guys' retreat into the soft Michigan summer night then turned to face her. His face remained inscrutable, but when he turned that sapphire gaze back to her, she had to reach back and grab the wall or risk doing something truly alarming, like fling herself at him.

Where in the hell had that come from?

She shook her head, took a step back. Before she could speak, he was in her space again, running a finger down her face, Gentle, but without a doubt, in complete control.

"Sorry Sara, I just couldn't help myself." His rough voice made her skin pebble. "Let's lock up here; you grab your stuff. We'll go somewhere for a drink."

He followed her inside the second set of doors, close enough so she could smell him – a new combination of soapy manliness, expensive cologne and lust. Her chest constricted. She had no business here, with him, reacting like that. Danger signals flashed in her vision. He reached up and flipped off the lights as she rounded the corner of the front desk on her way back to her office. She turned around to tell him not to bother with them; they kept that set on, and ran straight into his neck. He pulled her to him and muttered into her ear as she struggled to disentangle herself.

"Shh...wait. It's okay. I've got you." His hands moved from her head, to her neck, down her back and cupped her ass. She reached up to grasp his head and force his mouth back down to hers, making a near animal sound in her throat as their tongues collided. She twined her hands in his hair, felt her nipples harden, begging for his touch. Primal need rose in her, nearly painful, making her squirm and clutch him tighter.

His hand moved from her ass up to her shirt; reaching up, under the simple tank top she wore, straight to her bra. Wishing she still had on her lacy one, all that was lost in a haze of lust when he brushed his fingers against the fabric.

"Mmm, somebody is happy to see me," he whispered into her ear, causing a sudden nearly violent wetness in her shorts. She jerked away, leaving about a foot between them.

"What, baby?" He took a step back, passed a hand over his mouth. "Did I hurt you?"

Sara stared at what she could see of him, now that her eyes had adjusted to the gloom of the front office, and rubbed her arm nervously. *Patently insane – all of it.* They were in her office for

Christ's sake. She'd heard he liked to fuck around in public, but she didn't want to be another conquest. Her usually repressed nature struggled with her body's compulsion to have his hands on her, his mouth on hers, before she exploded. "Ah, no." Her voice wobbled, sounded thin to her own ears.

She turned away from him, hoping to marshal her strength and tell him to leave. As she made her way down the hallway she knew by heart even in the darkness, she could smell him on her and knew at that moment, without a doubt, she would fuck him, right then in the office.

They had been building towards it for too long. Her brain knew to keep quiet – it would not be heard over her body's clamor. Her baser need for him took over, and when he put a hand on her shirt and firmly tugged her back to him, she let him, shutting her eyes and praying she wasn't making a huge mistake.

She started to turn but he grabbed her from behind.

"Don't turn around," he whispered. "Let me show you what happens next. Just leave it all to me."

She relented and leaned back into his body. His lips claimed her neck. His hands rubbed both nipples at once. She bent her knees and moaned, raised her arms and put them behind her, around his head. He managed at some point to lose his expensive cufflinks and roll up his sleeves exposing tanned, strong forearms. He released each breast from their cup; caressed, rubbed, and pinched the aching hard nubs of sensitive flesh. His lips and teeth remained on her damp skin.

She began to move, rubbing against the heat of his erection pressed against her back. He groaned, and increased attention to her nipples, continued to use his lips to caress the back of her neck. A small fire burned wherever he touched her. She imagined she could come against the seam of her jeans, the pressure of his straining zipper against her, both of his hands on her nipples and his mouth in her ear and on her neck.

"Mmm... I have been dreaming of doing this to you for weeks." The words caused every nerve in her body to tingle. She closed her eyes.

He turned her around to face him, his hands on her upper arms. Before she could whimper about her poor lonely nipples he crushed his mouth on hers, pushing her up against the wall. Her left leg lifted and encircled his waist as her engorged clit begged for contact.

Oh my God, I am dry humping this grown man in my office.

He reached down and slowly unzipped her shorts, never removing his lips from the skin of her neck. He was muttering, something about "You smell exactly like I thought you would," but she couldn't be certain as her brain started fogging up like the inside of a car window, obscuring all rational thought.

Jack reached a hand down, brushed the outside of her panties. She moaned and leaned her head back against the wall. Sweat dripped slowly between her breasts as her breath caught in her throat. She sensed him grin against her skin as he leaned down to find the moisture and lap at it, his fingers lightly teasing her clit.

"Somebody *is* really happy to see me." His voice had an edge to it she loved.

Sara realized she was moving her hips, thrusting toward him as though drawn by a magnet. She started to reach down, needing to feel his flesh, but he grabbed her hands, lifted them up over her head, pinned her wrists against the wall.

"No, baby, let me. Just lean back and relax. I'm in charge."

Everything in her struggled against him, tried to resist, but the firm grasp he kept on her wrists was one of the most erotic sensations she'd ever experienced. She bit her lip as Jack slid her shorts down. He reached inside her panties, forming two of his fingers and thumb into a delicious double stimulator. Slowly, he moved against her swollen nub and slipped into her pussy as his lips traveled from her mouth, to her neck.

He manipulated her and maintained his control, seemingly without much effort, still holding her wrists captive over her head. She started lifting off, becoming as light as air, reaching the edge of extreme pleasure, while part of her tried to maintain her control. The man she'd been dreaming about for months was there, touching her, holding her captive against her office wall, and his lips, *dear God...* Eyes closed, head and arms up against the wall, she finally gave in to the pure, shuddering pleasure of it. Ignoring how much further she'd be willing to go with him; her usual reservations abandoned in his arms.

She rolled into her orgasm, as his fingers sank deep inside her and his thumb stayed pressed against her clit. She knew he was watching her, observing her reaction but didn't give a shit about that as she gave in to her body's clamor for release. Until that exact moment she had no idea how much she'd missed the pure, breathtaking beauty of an earth-shattering climax. Could she hang onto it, bottle it, so she could re-visit it after Jack was through with her?

She knew he had no intentions of doing anything beyond proving something to her against the wall in her office. But as far as she was concerned, he could prove all he wanted if it meant she could feel this way – every delicious, clutching, breathless minute of it. "Oh God, Jack." She heard her own whisper. Then he reached up and found that elusive bundle of nerves under her pubic bone and she exploded into a thousand shards of pure pleasure.

Her body pulsed with energy; she cried out as she yanked her wrists from his grasp and clenched his arm, her lips seeking his. He accommodated her with his warm mouth, delicious tongue and the grin she felt he must wear at every moment of the day.

"Oh yeah, you come just like I knew you would. I knew you'd grab me with that pussy and not let go," he muttered into her hair as she tried to calm her breathing. "Amazing." He sounded as breathless as she felt.

She sighed, rolled her head around, tried to get some semblance of dignity back. He kept his lips on her, on her shoulders, her neck, not willing to break contact. She reached for the zipper of his suit pants, admiring the view of his rumpled shirt and his tie released and askew. He leaned closer, placed both hands on the wall on either side of her head, closed his eyes and let her unhook his belt. His cock made an impressive mound underneath the boxer-type briefs. She licked her lips.

"Let's move in here," she muttered, and indicated her cubicle, reluctant to expose him in the hall. No matter that, she was standing there, her shorts flung aside and her shirt practically ripped off from behind.

"No." His voice was firm, used to being obeyed. She bit her lip. "Reach in there first, come on, Sara," He leaned back to allow her a better angle.

His animal maleness, his scent, now tinged with her own juices on his hand, the breathless way he spoke near her ear, all combined to bring out something completely new in her. Her nipples ached for his touch, her pussy clutched in post-orgasmic anticipation. Somewhere in the back of her mind, she could hear the sounds of the office at night. Sounds she was familiar with – the whirr of the fridge, the tick of the large art deco clock out front, even the traffic noises that were her usual backdrop for an evening work session. None of those things would ever sound the same to her again.

She stroked the head of his cock as it lunged out of his briefs, already slick with clear evidence of his desire. *So, he isn't all that much in control*, she thought as she reached lower to rub the length of him. She ran her hands down his thick shaft, which seemed to swell even more, filling her grip in a way that promised serious action.

"Mmm hmm. Very nice." He kept his eyes closed, his hands still planted on the wall. She reached down and cupped his balls, smiling as they drew up and contracted.

She brought her lips to his, their breathing combined as his increased. She shoved her tongue into his mouth. He closed his eyes and plunged his hands into her hair, moved his hips ever so slightly, and moaned deep in his throat, which sparked her own need to have him right then, inside her, before she exploded.

How crazy is this? He's a colleague, nearly forty years old, a guy you've been warned about by people who love you – and you're ready to let him fuck you like an animal standing up in the hallway?

Yes.

Some inner "New Sara" convinced her as she bent her knees and leaned over, taking in the scent of his most intimate and sensitive part, the raw, salty, musky man-smell. She flicked her tongue around the head, tasted him, allowed a little suction then withdrew to admire what she was sure would provide her a serious ride.

As she was about to suck the thick head back into her mouth, he grabbed her arms, tugged her straight up again, nearly growling with desire.

"I've been waiting since I first heard your voice on the phone. Tell me what you want," he demanded in a rough whisper.

Sara heard her voice as if listening in, unable to stop herself. "Please. Jack, fuck me. Now."

He pushed her firmly back against the wall, grabbing her leg to hike it up again and forced her lips open with his insistent tongue as he propped himself against the wall with one hand. He leaned into her, as the head of his cock reached towards her waiting and eager body.

A flick of his wrist, the sound of a condom being opened, and his hand on his cock indicated his readiness. She tried not to think about the fact that he had protection at his fingertips, as if he knew he would be getting some tonight. Those thoughts remained purely secondary to her urgent need for him inside of her.

"Now, give it to me right now," she hissed her demand as she wrapped her arms around his neck and plunged her hands into his thick hair.

"I will baby. Gotta go slow. Trust me." His breath tickled her ear. He reached down slid some combination of fingers into her aching body. She jerked and moaned as he used them to stretch her. She thrust against him, wanting more.

He reached around and grabbed her ass, pulled her closer and slowly eased into her, one delicious inch at a time. She stretched, accommodating his girth, her body spreading and accepting him. She gasped, her eyes widening as his thickness filled her. Up on her tiptoes, one leg wrapped firmly around his waist providing an amazing angle, she sighed with satisfaction. He finally pressed his full length inside her pulsing walls, his pubic bone jammed hard against the pulsing nub of her clit.

She moaned as he withdrew, eased himself away, the extreme emptiness he left behind making her gasp. He looked into her eyes and reached down to cup her breast in the hand that wasn't propped against the wall for support. Keeping the head of his lovely thick shaft inside, he caressed her nipple, tweaking it, murmuring something she couldn't hear. Sweat trickled down her back.

"Jack, please. . ."

"What, Sara."

"I need you back inside me." she paused. "I need your cock again." Every nerve ending in her body tingled with anticipation of his lips covering hers, of his cock spreading her, filling her completely.

He obliged, firmly, faster this time. She lifted her leg up higher around his waist to allow for more contact, and groaned at the extreme sensation of his body inside hers. He began to move against her, in and out, deliciously slow. His breath picked up and he grabbed her ass again, pulling her tighter to his body. He made a low sound deep in his throat.

She turned her head to the right, caught their reflection in the glass door of the kitchen. His tall body, still mostly dressed attached to hers, one hand on the wall, her leg wrapped around his waist as her body matched him thrust for thrust. She closed her eyes, but the image burned there like a brand.

"Shit woman, you are gonna make me come like a teenager," he muttered above her head, his neck pressed into her face. She tried to get the picture of him on his bus ads out of her head – tan, handsome, grinning at the world – holy shit but *he* could make her feel like *this*?

"Fuck me harder – oh my God, Jack!" she reached around to grasp his ass and shove him back inside. Her standing leg spasmed, as her pussy clutched at him, in a seemingly continuous wave of pleasure. The pressure his pubic bone put on her clit as he moved his amazing thickness in and out, making that deep sound in his throat, the feel of her ass against the wall, the sheer thrill of doing it right there, in the darkened hallway of her office, raced through her. She let it take her, realizing her mistake too late – the mistake of letting Jack into her body and into her life.

Sweat beaded up on his face. It was slick under her fingers as she reached up to pull his mouth to hers. She wanted to smell him, taste him while she came – needed to feel him closer, wanted him to see what he did to her. She grabbed his hair in her attempt to get him ever closer as her entire body flushed with blood in the onrush of serious orgasmic bliss. She had a sudden need to make him lose control – needed to wipe that fucking grin off his face once as he gave a final thrust and groaned. Thrilled when that cocky grin was replaced with a look she recognized as one she'd been wearing earlier. His lips covered hers at the last moment, blinding her with the full sensation of his whole self, inside, covering her, marking her as his.

He shuddered as he thrust deep and released. Her body pulsed, grabbed and held him deeper. He continued to move against her as her clit stayed swollen and sensitized. She put her hands on his shoulders, still encased in that dress shirt, observed that his tie was still on, and sighed.

"OK, wow, um, I don't usually act like this," she said quietly as she admired the hardness of his shoulders under her hands.

"Yeah, well, you just needed somebody to show you how fun this can be." His voice stayed low as he withdrew and leaned down to kiss her neck, near her ear.

"So now is the embarrassing part, right?" Sara had no confidence in her knees whatsoever as she gripped the wall and willed her body calm.

"What? Hell, no, I'm not embarrassed. I feel great." He pulled off the condom, tucked himself back inside his pants, zipped them up then ducked into the kitchenette. He came back carrying some paper towels.

She took the stack from him and turned away. She was used to handling the clean-up part post-sex in private, but what the hell, the New Sara could wipe up in front of the guy who made her wet. Jack smoothed his shirt and rolled down his sleeves. He glanced around and grabbed her shorts from where she had flung them about two feet down the hall and handed them to her.

"Let's go get something to eat – I'm starved." He grinned as she shook her head, clearing the cobwebs placed there by the very fact of what she had done, in that hall with the guy who never even came out of his tie or his thousand-dollar shoes. She also felt great, truthfully, but somehow that seemed wrong.

The turn of a key startled them both.

"Shit, shit, shit." Sara zipped up her shorts and cast about for her sandals.

"Um, babe, tuck in your shirt in the back," Jack whispered. "You look like you just got fucked against the office wall."

He grinned at her, blue eyes snapping with something Sara could not identify. When he turned away and ran his hand through his dark hair, it stood up in way that made her want to thread her fingers through it.

God – it could get interesting if every time he spoke, her pussy spoke back.

Get a grip Sara. Do not let him do this to you.

"Yeah, thanks, whatever," she mumbled, as she made her way back to her office to flip the light on.

Jack ambled into the kitchenette, opened the fridge and grabbed a Diet Coke

"Who's here?" the sing-song voice of Meg, the office sad-sack agent, traveled back to them.

"Just me Meg," Sara shocked herself with her voice's steadiness.

"Well, young lady, did you buy a new car or something?"

Meg didn't do much business, never had. She hung out around the office all the time, never going out to work. Most offices had them – the resident sob-story types that managers could not cut lose out of the goodness of their hearts. She was also a great listener which endeared her to many agents and kept her from being completely annoying.

"No lovely lady," Jack called out striding out to the hall. "That's my ride as you well know!"

"Jaaack, you devil!" Meg voice scraped fingernails down Sara's internal chalkboard.

Sara rolled her eyes. She suddenly felt really, really cheap. Jack flirted with everybody. He hadn't singled her out on the phone over the last few weeks. Flirting for him was like breathing; he couldn't *not* do it.

Great. And you let him fuck you, practically in public, without a second thought. What is wrong with you?

Nothing, the New Sara caressed her ear. *Nothing another session with him won't cure. Enjoy. Don't think; don't plan. Just lay back and take what he has to give you.*

Jack met Meg halfway up the hall, and Sara realized he headed her off on purpose, keeping her from approaching where the hall smelled a bit musky. There would be no doubt that sex had occurred there.

"What brings you to our fancy downtown office, young man?"

"Had to bring something over to Sara. We have a tough deal that's finally coming together. I wanted to deliver it in person and I knew she'd be here – she's always here, isn't she?" Jack threw an arm around Meg's shoulders.

"Yes, our Sara, she's a hard worker," Meg agreed. "She'll be our top producer in no time!"

Jack looked back, caught Sara's eye and winked. "Yep, she'll be on top very soon for sure, especially if I have a say in it!"

She glared at him, her whole body reacting to his words like a silly love-struck teenager.

"We're headed out," Sara caught up with them and breezed past. "Want us to lock up or are you staying a while Meg?" She didn't care, really, simply needed to get out of the space. Her brain spun out of control. It was not a feeling she liked or wanted to perpetuate. "Meet you at Tres Amigos Jack." She tossed over her shoulder, unwilling to look back, not trusting herself to meet his eyes.

On his way to meet Sara at the Mexican place, Jack had to roll down all his windows and let the slightly cooling Michigan summer night breeze ruffle his hair. He kept a hand on the wheel but brought the other to his face, wanting to keep Sara's scent near.

He shook his head to clear it. There had been no need to drop any papers off – that was what scanners and email were for. He had wanted her to think it a random drop-in visit, not the premeditated encounter it was. But things had spiraled out of control fast, too fast.

It had been a real buzz getting to know her through this deal. Her professionalism, the calm efficiency she used to handle her buyer had been amazing, and he knew damn good and well that was part of her appeal. It drove him to her office tonight, determined to scoop her up and take her out, somewhere, anywhere, dinner, dancing, whatever she wanted. The sight of her in unselfconsciously sexy denim and cotton, hair unruly, sans any makeup, eyes bright and obviously eager to see him – had smacked him in square in the libido. He licked his lips in the car's dark interior.

The chemical spark that passed between them when she took the innocuous excuse of a document had caught Jack off guard. He thrived on raw sexual energy. He'd spent years enjoying the company of as many different women as possible – as teacher and student. But this? This was something completely new to him. The ever-present hum of erotic energy running through him lately revved, and his brain filled with images of them together, of her on her knees eyes cast down. His hands shook as he readjusted them on the wheel.

What was it about this chick anyway? She was hot, no doubt – tight ass, firm body, soft brown hair that he could still feel between his fingers. And those absolutely incredible eyes. Unlike many men, he had no preference: blondes, redheads, brunettes, made no difference. He tended to be drawn to women on the thinner side or at least ones that cared about their bodies enough to exercise every now and then, which she clearly did.

It had been nearly a year since he first saw her – really saw her – when she walked out of that penthouse condo, wearing that fine, just-fucked look on her lovely face. A solid year and his obsession with her had only increased. Usually, when a woman proved to be inaccessible he moved on to the next one. Not this time.

The evening hadn't gone at all like he had planned. Figuring she'd be dressed for work and would want to go out he had come straight from his own office and had the night planned from start to finish, not really anticipating his need to take her, right then and there. Something about her had forced him closer, only for a taste. Of course, he'd gotten a lot more than that. Her meeting his need halfway only served to ramp up his urge to take, to own, up against the wall like an animal.

Her early hesitation and shyness reinforced what his research had predicted. The lovely woman had gone a while without a man's touch. It had only made him want her even more. The usual, smug, self-satisfied feeling eluded him and it pissed him off. That coupled with the twitchy need to have her again, to make her beg for him, made him embarrassed and horny in equal measure.

Shit. What the hell, Gordon?

Jack ran a hand through his hair. He sensed she still had pent up energy. He wanted to release it; wanted more than anything to prove he was the man to do it. But he'd be damned if, for the first time in years, he hadn't let himself go. Allowed himself orgasm without consciously keeping his distance. When she had reached up to capture his lips at the last moment, he hadn't even tried to resist. He'd wanted to be completely aware of her as he shared the ultimate connection; her scent, her hair, her lips. It was as if she knew he normally resisted contact at that moment. He had clutched her ass with one hand and relished the firm feel of her skin and muscle underneath as her amazing walls continued to spasm and contract along the length and width of him. It hit him hard, in his gut and between the eyes, not only in his cock.

When she'd gotten embarrassed again after they were done, he'd had to move away from her, or risk acting like a sap. She had looked devastating – her hair disheveled in the back, her color high, and her lips swollen from his kisses. It was one of his favorite looks on a woman – the "Well Fucked by Jack Gordon" face. He knew it well. He would gladly have picked her up and plunked her down on the floor and given it to her again and again to get that connected feeling back. It warred inside him, the need to possess and please, to control and satisfy, all at the same time.

He shook his head once again as he pulled into the parking lot outside the restaurant. *Get hold of yourself man. She's just another pussy – a pretty sweet one at that. You've managed to break that office in, enjoy the afterglow!* He smiled as she pulled in behind him and eased out of her car, long, sexy legs leading the way. *Damn, the woman was hot.* He held out an arm, she took it with a skeptical look and they walked into the restaurant together.

"Here," Jack held the dark ring of a jalapeño to Sara's lips.

"I can feed myself, thanks." She grabbed one from her plate to pop into her mouth. He shrugged and ate the hot pepper he'd been holding, without taking his eyes from hers.

She was no lightweight, but after only two beers felt tipsy. *Drunk on Jack – his proximity, his voice, and the lips that he kept brushing against her neck.* The fact that he'd ordered for them without even asking her what she wanted didn't have its usual effect on her either. She loved it.

He'd ordered exactly what she was craving – a dark Mexican beer and the hottest possible burrito smothered in rich tomato sauce. He regaled her with stories from his recent string of real estate failures while they ate. At one point she had laughed so hard she'd let out a snort which made him laugh even harder.

At that moment he put an arm around her and pulled her close, so close she could smell him and she had to close her eyes to battle her desire to climb up on his lap. He soothed, felt familiar but dangerous and elusive at the same time. She knew he couldn't, or wouldn't, be into her any more than any other woman. He had to be the absolute worst man she could get attached to – a self-centered, man-whore, intent on his own satisfaction every minute of the day.

He didn't let go of her and she tilted her face up to his to receive his lips. His kiss made the room disappear, then spin. She couldn't resist the temptation to grab his thigh, pressed against hers. He grinned against her lips as she ran her hand up near his swelling zipper.

"I think I'm going to like this new Sara," He broke away and whispered, not stopping her hand's journey.

She stared at him, her mission towards his crotch forgotten. How in the hell could he know that she felt herself splitting in two –

becoming an Old and a New Sara. Old Sara would have never fucked him like that, but this new creature loved how he made her feel, and wanted it again. Her life would forever be divided in her mind between "before Jack" and "after Jack." The concept that he had so much control over her already pissed her off immensely.

"Yeah, well, New Sara needs some sleep," she insisted and glanced at her watch. "Busy day tomorrow and all." He threw enough cash down for the bill and tip and held out his hand to ease her out of their booth. She took it, loving the already familiar heat of his flesh.

It took everything she had not to invite him back to her place. He didn't seem inclined once their meal was complete anyway. Instead, she adopted his breezy manner, gave him a peck on the check and climbed into her car. Jack shut her door, motioned for her to roll down the window. She knew she should escape, but did not want to leave. He leaned into her open window, grabbed her by the back of the neck and guided her lips to his for a better good night kiss. New Sara made promises with her mouth. Beer, and a slight echo of salsa, ghosted across her taste buds. He broke away, touched her on the nose.

"See you soon, yes?"

"See you soon, Jack, yes." She started up her car. The throaty motor of the Beemer gave her a thrill.

"Oh, and stop buying these foreign cars, will ya?" he grinned. "This is Michigan you know – buy American!"

He turned and disappeared into the night.

Jack had used every bit of his resolve not to invite her back to his house. He would have given anything to lower her down onto his king-sized bed and make her sing with pleasure, to cry out for him again and again. His cock stirred at the thought of it. He made a mental note to dig some of his toys out of the wooden chest buried in the back of his closet. Strips of worn leather, a blindfold and a few other choice items danced around in his brain. Thinking he'd never use them again after the last woman had nearly screamed with shock when he suggested it, he'd hidden them and his darker urges away.

With Sara, they had come surging back, nearly suffocating him with need. White knuckling the wheel with one hand, he cranked the stereo with the other, hoping to drive some of the clamor in his head out. Dear God but he wanted more from her. More than she might be bargaining for.

Something told him to wait, to save that for another time. Let her sleep on the office quickie; see how much more she could take. He had a feeling she'd be back. He sensed himself settling back into a familiar place. A place where he knew his heart would be safe and his body satisfied. He had to maintain control of the situation, and he would. Something in him remained unable to shake the uncertainty. She would not be just another woman, and that kept him up all night pondering the possibilities of Sara.

CHAPTER FIVE

Sara didn't hear from Jack for nearly ten days. Since the tough part of their deal had essentially ended, she had assumed he'd moved on to other deals, other clients and other agents. She tried not to let that disappoint her, but it did. Tried not to admit how she awoke nearly every single night with his name on her lips and moisture between her thighs. She was not about to reach out to him – no way. New Sara was not happy about it, but that was too bad. Control had to be maintained with a guy like him.

When he finally called, she ignored him. He didn't leave a message or call back. At night, alone in bed, she spent many hours reliving that hot night in the hallway and tried to use her own fingers to recreate what he did, to bring herself to such a shuddering, earth-shaking climax. It never worked.

Being pissed off at the man had become a full-time job which made her even madder at herself. Trying to focus, to channel some of that energy into work, did help. When she realized she could credit him for that too, it made her want to throw something heavy through a window.

Sara got to Sunday and did the usual prep for her Open House. One of her white elephant listings was a funky, sixties-built, raised ranch, in a premium location overlooking the Huron River. It boasted an amazing one-hundred-eighty-degree view of the river and park below from the wall of windows across the back. A screened-in porch on the side of the house afforded an even more panoramic vista.

She had it listed for eight hundred thousand, insanity, she knew, but it came with three acres and it would make an incredible building lot if the new owners couldn't tolerate its current choppy floor plan. The sellers were friends of hers; a couple she went to college with, who'd gotten married right away and launched into a whirlwind of reproduction with two kids nearly within a year of each other and were now expecting a third. Sometimes she did wonder what it would be like to actually care about someone so much you'd want to carry his child and raise it together. As usual, Jack's striking face shot through her brain before she banished it.

Open houses sucked, generally. They rarely yielded anything more useful than a good nap but she got the place ready. Brochures, business cards and fresh flowers strategically arranged on tables. Anger rose, nearly choking her, as irrational images of Jack kissing another woman passed in front of her vision.

Snap out of it! Focus. Sell this damn house today or at least snag a new buyer who can afford it.

The temperamental alarm system got a final once-over to make sure it would not go blasting off when a potential buyer entered the house from the side door instead of the front like it had the last time she held this one open. Sara caught her image in the front hall mirror. Ralph Lauren tan trousers, bright teal linen top, high-heeled open-toed Ferragamos, freshly pedicured feet, light makeup and lipstick – check – ready to roll.

Two o'clock became two forty-five with no guests. No big surprise. She made it through half of her water and a few chapters of the latest hot vampire novel she'd brought with her to pass the time. Bored, she got up to walk around, stretching her legs, when she saw a car pull into the long gravel drive.

She watched as Jack unfolded his tall frame out of the corvette and walked around to reach into the passenger's seat. It struck her that she had never seen him in anything but a suit, or at least dress pants, shirt and tie, as she admired his ass in the dark jeans. He looked good enough to eat. Sara pressed her thighs together in anticipation.

Panic replaced her blooming desire. Surely, he didn't think she would leave her open house an hour early.

What was he doing at her open house? Was there a problem with their deal?

She glimpsed a shopping bag from Whole Foods in one hand. He grinned at her, lighting up his arresting eyes. Her breath caught in her throat.

Shit.

She had made a vow to herself she would not get caught up in the Jack Gordon whirlwind. However, here she was, high and mighty, and yet about to explode with need for his lips on hers.

Double shit. She sighed.

"I thought you might be lonely all the way out here and we should have a picnic, what do you say?" He made his way to the front door. He wore a plain burgundy T-shirt, jeans that hugged his front as nicely as his rear, and driving shoes. Momentarily blinded by lust, she fought the impulse to pull him into the foyer and make him fuck her until she was spent.

Nice, very nice. The guy brings you a picnic and you want to skip right to the after-play?

Turning on her heel, she headed back into the house without even responding to his suggestion, assuming he would follow her. Sara realized she had to get control of herself before talking or her voice would surely betray her blatant desire. She glanced at her watch. Three p.m.; she had to focus on her job for one more hour. Let him wait.

"Don't you have an open house of your own?" She sounded a tad more irritable than she intended.

"Nope." He walked right into her personal space, brushed her hair out of her face and kissed her. His firm lips remained noncommittal. She shivered, and he kept his hand on her neck, under her hair. He caressed her almost absentmindedly as he looked around at the house.

"Well, the view is great," he admitted, as he strode into the front bedroom suite. Sara watched as he strolled out of that room, looking at the high cathedral ceilings made of light ash wood. He whistled, picked up his grocery bag and walked into the kitchen. His quick eyes took in the skylights, the new gleaming stainless steel appliances, and tile floor.

"Nice, but it's sort of cold in here, isn't it? Maybe some color, some flowers or something would help?"

"Fuck off Jack; I don't need your help. Why are you here anyway?"

"Easy, tiger, easy," he leaned on the counter top. "I know you know what to do. I can't help it. It's second nature for me to say something about the house first." Sara caught herself clenching and unclenching her fists, and stopped. *Damn the man anyway.* She couldn't even stay mad at him. She slumped against the doorframe.

"It's a shit listing. I don't get any showings and hardly any new buyers from these open houses. The sellers could care less that it sits here and gets stale," she sighed. She relaxed, only to have her desire for him rush over her like a tidal wave, so she moved away hoping that would help. He attended to his grocery bag and began setting stuff on the counter.

"What the hell am I going to do when a guest shows up, Jack? Put that crap away."

"It's okay babe, we'll just say we rolled out the red carpet for your potential buyers with these nice strawberries and cream. He pulled the last container from the bag with a flourish.

"You are insane, you know that?" She stared at the array of stuff on the counter.

"You won't think that when I show you this amazing bottle of wine I found. I forgot I had it." He pulled out a green bottle with a French label of some sort, two wine glasses, and a corkscrew.

"Um, yeah, well, I'm not really comfortable doing this here, I mean, it's not my kitchen." Sara stammered as she took another step away from him to get his smell out of her nose.

"Sure it is." He worked the cork out allowing her to admire the amazing definition of his arms. "I'll bet you've spent more time in this fucked-up house with its million-dollar view than you have in your own house since you listed it. I mean, you do opens, you refill sales brochures, you check on the lawn, what else? Tell me I'm wrong." He pulled the cork free, splashed some golden liquid into each glass and handed one to her. By the time he'd completed the task, Sara had made her way nearly six feet from him.

"Baby, I don't bite," he coaxed, as he held out the glass to her.

She surged forward, as if to prove she wasn't afraid, grabbing the glass as she passed.

"Thanks. Never had a happy hour at an open house."

Sara positioned herself at the far end of the room, as far from Jack as she could get. She faced out to the river and contemplated her options. On the one hand, her body declared its intention, pussy officially soaking wet, her nipples so hard they ached. Her skin quivered in anticipation of what his plans included for a "picnic," in a house where she didn't even feel welcome to use the bathroom, much less host some sort of kinky food-sex session. She glanced at him, standing so calm and collected while every inch of her skin flushed and her heart deafened her with its pounding.

Her hand shook as she raised the glass to her lips. She really should tell him to get the hell out of there. The situation was headed in a very dangerous direction and not because it was pretty obvious he had come here for one reason only. His sheer chemistry spoke volumes to hers. She knew what he wanted. The clarity of that realization calmed her. Looking back out at the river, she tried to slow her breathing. A familiar feeling stole over her. It was an annoying slip of focus, much like when she'd been absorbed with Adam just last year. How in the world could one man turn her on and piss her off so completely by standing on the other side of the room? It simply wasn't fair.

Jack stayed quiet. He stared out the window alongside her, sipping his wine, his breathing calm and controlled.

"What's the basement like?" he asked. "I mean, are there more rooms down there? There is really only one bedroom on this main floor – that's a tough sell, even with this view."

"Uh, yeah, there are two beds and two more full baths down, plus another great room, a walk out with an enormous fireplace." Sara muttered, brain fuzzy from the shift in conversation. She glanced at her watch. Three twenty-five. About another half hour and they could lock this place up and be on their way.

She watched him without trying to stare. He was truly larger than life, and he knew it. Tall, exotically Celtic – "Black Irish" with his raven's wing hair and blue eyes, seemingly ever-present stubble – he soaked up the energy in any room he entered. His torso was V-shaped and strong, with prominent muscle definition in his arms, shoulders and back, leading down to a completely grab-able ass, strong masculine thighs and calves. She let her eyes travel downward, along his arm that held the wine glass.

Her thighs started to quiver again so she took a step back from the window. Her brain started to close down. The dark blue of the jeans hugged his ass in way she wished her hands could. It took every ounce of self-control she possessed not to cross the room, drop to her knees in front of him, release that amazing cock and… Sara shut her eyes and pictured them in the hallway of her office again with her back shoved up against the wall and his cock sunk deep inside her. She shivered.

Jack downed his glass, crossed back into the kitchen. She waited for a count of ten and saw him emerge, carrying a tray of strawberries from God knows where.

"This view is the best part of this piece of shit house," he declared. "Let's not waste it."

Speechless, she followed him out onto the screened porch where he plopped the tray down on a small square table. A couple of ratty chairs crouched on either side of it. He motioned for her to sit next to him and began dipping the strawberries into the bowl of cream.

"Sit back Sara," he insisted, in that low voice she remembered so well from the hallway. "Relax. Work time is over."

"B-b-but, it's not four o'clock yet." The pulse between her legs took on a life of its own as she watched him.

New Sara spoke – *Fuck the open house. Let's see what he has planned. You know it will be worth it.*

"OK, but wait, let me lock it up and set the alarm." She dashed out of the room under his bemused gaze, locked all four doors, and set the alarm. When she returned and sat back down in the chair, she kicked off her shoes, ready for his next move. He held out a hand. She took it and let him tug her onto his lap.

"Here, have one of these strawberries," he said, as he handed her one drenched in cream. She took the fruit without breaking eye contact with him. She ignored her brain as it once again tried to raise a protest and let herself drown in their sapphire blue pools.

She licked the cream slowly dripping down her fingers. His eyes widened and he captured her hand, brought it to his lips. The sensation of him sucking the crème off made her gasp and moisture flood her panties. The lovely press of his erection against her bottom didn't help. He released her but kept his gaze steady on hers as he dipped another strawberry bringing the sweet concoction to her lips.

Shit. It was some sort of triple cream. Something she hadn't allowed herself to eat for years. *Incredible. Delicious.* The strawberries exploded in her mouth at every bite with bright, sweet flavor. She chewed, swallowed, and nodded at him to give her another.

His grin at her eagerness to get at them, to lick them, and to gorge herself on their bounty didn't even bother her. When he pressed his lips to hers, she had the amazing feeling that she had been kissing him, tasting him, forever. She sighed as he put his hands on her waist and lifted her up. She started to turn and straddle him, aching with need for him to fill her again.

"No." He made her stand all the way up. "Go sit over there." She did, obeying in a way that went against her fundamental resistance to being bossed around. When he pulled her foot onto his lap and sunk his knuckles into her instep, she groaned and leaned her head back. The release of tension in her neck and back seemed directly proportional to the spot on her foot he chose to rub.

"Oh, Jesus," she muttered, easing herself down further in the chair, allowing more of her leg onto his lap, coming closer to the growing bulge in those amazing jeans.

He continued to caress her foot, stopping only long enough to hand her freshly dipped strawberries. The combined sensations of the rich, sweet, and tart morsels along with the relaxation he was creating via her foot were nearly too much. She started to sit up, worried about losing control, yet again, to Jack's magic. Her brain tried to break through the fog of horniness. It reminded her that, of all men on the planet, this one she really ought not toy with. It could only end in disaster.

At that moment, the alarm boomed through the house.

"Fuck!" She lurched up, knocking over her wine glass.

"It's cool, I'll see what it is." Jack stood seemingly unaware of the impressive bulge he had on display and walked over to the door of the screened porch.

Sara sat and took long, deep breaths, willing herself calm. Jack was a professional and had been at this job way longer than she. He could handle whatever it was.

It took about fifteen minutes for him to come back into the porch.

"What," She winced at the squeakiness in her voice. "Did someone want to see the house?"

"Yeah," he laughed, "you forgot to pull in your signs when you locked the place up. These poor saps thought they could walk right in and so they did. I showed them around, made an appointment to meet with them tomorrow to discuss other options. Sweet couple," he smirked.

"You utter asshole," Sara jumped to her feet, prepared to call this little rendezvous finished – *the man had stolen her buyers*. He simply could not turn it off, could he? Her brain cheered her on – *run away, get as far away from him as you can and stay there; it's for your own good.*

He intercepted her on her way to the door.

"Hold on, hold on, we'll share them I swear," he declared.

"You know what Jack, fuck you. Get out of here. This is nuts." His eyes narrowed. She crossed her arms and tried to still her pounding heart. His dark gaze pinned her, intent and sexy as hell. She took a breath but as she started to order him out again, he pulled her close, covered her protests with lips and plunged his tongue into her mouth. Walking her backwards a few steps he propped against the wall, and kissed her with an intensity that made the room spin. She tried her best but couldn't resist burying her hands in his thick hair and arch her body into his. He broke the kiss and took her arms from around his neck without a word.

"Take your clothes off. All of them." His voice was rough, low and brooked no argument.

She started to cross her arms again but he yanked them over her head, pinning her against the wall as he had done that night in her office. The cloud of lust that surrounded her parted, leaving room only for bright clear fury. His lips were centimeters from hers. His strong body pressed into hers, compelling in her ways she didn't know existed. *I can't let him do this.* She licked her lips, encouraging him to come closer.

"Ow! Son of a..." he stepped away holding a hand over his mouth. Sara's body shook and she had to sink to her heels. She could taste blood and knew she'd bitten hard, and meant it. But her brain had shut down on her now, leaving her alone with regret and a sharp kernel of unmet need. She knew at that moment she'd do whatever he wanted. She had to, somehow, although part of her tried to fight it. He pulled her to her feet, gentle, his eyes concerned.

"Trust me. Take them off Sara." He leaned in before she could move away and licked her lower lip, letting her know she was forgiven, before stepping back.

Her hands shook as she slid the zipper down the front of her blouse, slipped her trousers off her hips. If he thought she'd be intimidated by this, he had another thing coming. The breeze kicked through the screen, bringing a welcomed chill to her overheated flesh. She raised her chin and flipped the clasp on her bra, hooked a finger through her panties. Hesitating just a minute, long enough for him to give a nearly imperceptible nod, she slid them down her legs and stood up, trying not to cross her arms over her nudity.

"Dear God you are exquisite." He breathed, not moving from his spot nearly two feet away. She sensed something, something she would come to associate with a darkness deep in him that she wanted more than anything to lighten, as long as he shared it with her, and only her.

Mine. The voice started out small, but got steadily louder in her brain. *Mine?* Oh hell, she was really screwed.

Jack swallowed, took a breath, and came to terms with what he wanted to do to the woman standing there, glorious, naked and…his. He shook his head. No, she was just there. In no way whatsoever was she "his." His chest tightened as he closed the gap between them and ran a hand down her cheek, neck, across her collarbones, and cupped one breast as his thumb brushed the hard nipple. She shuddered but didn't move.

He cupped her neck with his other hand and pulled her close, slanted his lips over hers and dove into her mouth, lazy, slow, and easy but stopped when she started to touch him.

"No. Hands down. I'm touching. You are just letting me." She frowned but he smiled, and kissed her forehead. "It's okay Sara. Let it go. Let me do this. You won't be sorry I promise you."

Jack felt the dark control steal over him, taking him, as he ran his hands over his woman's body while she stood, trembling; eyes trained on his. His soul longed for more, to take, own and possess in ways he had never experienced. His balls ached, his cock was so hard, and he knew if she touched him now he'd likely come all over himself like a teenager.

He teased the hard nubs of her nipples with both thumbs, licked her lips then owned her mouth once more. The small sounds she made drove him insane but he kept control, held back. "I'm going to make you come Sara, but you can't until I tell you. Do you understand? If you do, I'm leaving and you can't do any of the touching I know you want to do." He cradled her face in his hands. Her eyes were wide and her breathing fast. He could smell her need, her lust, and it made him grit his teeth against the urgency to toss her on the floor and fuck her. No. He had to do this. He had to see if he still could dominate, and, more importantly, if she would submit.

She shook, and he folded her into his arms. "Shh, it's okay. It's going to be fine." He brushed a strand of hair from her eyes.

"You have to let me be in control." She nodded. He stepped back and slipped his belt loose from the loops never taking his eyes from hers. The lust spiraled through his brain, nearly blinding him, but he held on. "On your knees," he kept his voice soft remembering the last time he'd tried this what a disaster that had turned out to be. "Now." He slapped his palm with the leather.

She did as she was told. He brought a chair around to face her. "Put your elbows here on the seat, and give me your wrists."

"Jack," her voice was breathy. "I don't know..." He knelt beside her and threaded his fingers in her hair.

"But I do, Sara. I won't hurt you. I swear it. I am however, going to rock your world in ways you have only imagined until now," He tilted her head back, holding tight and kissed her, hard, then broke away. "Give me your wrists." Taking a deep breath, she propped her elbows on the chair seat, shivering when he fastened the soft leather around them, binding her without really fastening anything to gauge her response. "Tell me a word. Any word. As long as I know it. You say that word and I stop whatever I'm doing."

She whimpered and shifted her knees. He hesitated, but then crouched behind her, ran his hands down her bare shoulders, back and to her narrow waist. His hand grazed her ass, the smooth creamy skin tempting him, begging for his handprint.

The loud smack of flesh on flesh made him tingle and her cry out. He clutched her hair again leaning in close. "A word, baby. Any word. Tell me now."

"Emerson." She whispered and moaned as he pressed against her, his cock ready to explode in his jeans. He lowered his lips to her shoulder, ran his tongue up her delicious neck.

"Emerson it is." He bit down, just hard enough to make her flinch then groan as he sucked on her skin. His hand connected with her ass once more, hard, but he knew not too hard. Just enough. Then again, finding a virgin expanse of flesh to tantalize. Then once more, making her squirm against him. He held her close with his other arm, still tasting her neck and shoulders, loving the salty essence of her sweat and the smell of her arousal that grew with every contact.

He pressed her over the chair, forcing her bound arms forward, exposing her bare ass, and groaned at the sight of her angry red skin, ran both hands down her hips and ground his still covered cock into the delectable cleft of her ass. She tilted her hips up, welcomed him and sighed. He reached around and pinched one nipple, then the other, not gentle, waiting to see how she reacted before moving further. "Oh hell yes, I knew you'd like this. How did I know, hmmm?" He leaned over her, using his fingers like clamps, pinching and relishing her moans.

"Oh God, Jack, please," her voice muffled against her arm. He let go of her then, ran both hands down her waist once more then reached around and touched her sex.

"Please what baby? Please what?" He licked his way down her spine, sucking in deep breaths of her, using his finger to press against her engorged and needy clit. "Remember Sara, you can't come. Not until I tell you." He put his entire hand over her mound, felt the heat and wet there then heard a moan but bit down on his tongue when he realized it came from him.

She was so perfect – and so his. She wiggled under his hand. His breath came in short gasps, his balls tightened, readying his body for release. He pressed in with one finger, slipped inside her and felt her pulse all around him.

"Please…" her voice pleased him. "I need," She sucked in a deep breath.

He withdrew the finger, brought it to her lips so she could taste herself. She sucked hard, making his hips jerk as his body reacted before his brain could reestablish control. "You ready to come baby?" He'd forgotten how difficult this was. How challenging to please before being pleased, to hold someone's ultimate trust in your hands. He drew back, brought his lips to her upturned ass and lapped at the beautiful pink of her pussy. She squealed and spread her legs further. As he slid two fingers into her dripping body, she sighed. "Come Sara, come now!" He reared up and unzipped his jeans grabbed his aching rod and gave it a few jerks. Didn't take much.

"Jack! Yes! Please oh God…Jack." Her voice, her lips forming the sounds of his name as her body bucked and pulsed around his fingers, made the room narrow to a black space where he stood, poised on the edge of a cliff, one well-shod foot ready to make a leap, about to jump again, as his cock gushed and covered his hand and Sara's ass. At that moment he saw her, Jenna, the woman he'd experimented with in law school. The one who'd taught him what it meant to master another person, right before she fucked both his roommates and laughed in his face when he'd tried to propose.

Jack pulled his body away, sat back on heels staring at Sara's amazing still pink skin, her ass and the slick fluid coating her thighs. She did love this. He'd known it somehow. His head suddenly ached with long suppressed memory. Sara squirmed under his gaze. "Jack?" He took a breath. He couldn't do this. Not to her. It was not a road he would travel, not again.

"Baby, I'm sorry." He helped her up, released her wrists and pulled her in for a gentle kiss. She wrapped herself around him, fisted her hands in his hair, returning the kiss so hard and fast he got dizzy from it combined with the quick way he'd climaxed. "I'm sorry," he whispered into her hair, as he held her close, his brain on fire and his body not far behind.

Sara's skin burned, starting at the sting of her ass and ending with the blaze in her brain. How in God's name had he done that to her – made her give in and so turned on at the same time? She let him hold her as her body started to shiver. Held her until she calmed, whispering "I'm sorry's" the whole time. She finally looked up at him. His face was a mask of agony and frustration. Frowning she pushed back from the comforting strength of his chest.

"What's with the sorry? That was, um, incredible." Her ears got hot. She had never, ever been handled like that. Never felt the fucking earth move under her feet. She couldn't understand why he seemed so upset.

Perhaps she shouldn't have let him. He was obviously unhappy with the whole thing. Maybe she should be too, but the thought that they could do this and more together made her bite her lip to keep from begging him to take her home, to play with her more, to possess her like he seemed to want.

Already mentally typing "BDSM" into a Google search, she stared at him, amazed at her body's reaction to this jerk who had stolen perfectly good clients right out from under her nose then ordered her around like, like…

Oh hell, and you'd let him hadn't you? Yes you did. Jesus.

She wiped herself off with a napkin, found her clothes and tugged them back on in silence, determined to rebuff him, reject his little power play. But found herself wanting more, needing something to reassure her. She held back tears, unwilling to let on how much he'd affected her. As she stared, his eyes darkened to a deeper sapphire.

Struck by their intensity, she realized she hadn't really seen them in the hot office hallway last week. They were one of his most incredibly sexy assets and he used them well.

She stood, arms crossed, her pussy still twitching with residual pleasure. He sighed, ran a hand over his eyes. "Sit." He pointed to a chair. She raised an eyebrow.

"Sorry, no. Playtime is over." She started to pick up the discarded strawberry tops and put them on the tray. He gripped her arm, the look on his face causing her to sink into the chair, protests dying on her lips. He sat across from her, gripping her hands.

"I didn't mean to," he stopped and looked down at the floor. "I hope I didn't hurt you." She stared at him. "It won't happen again." Before she could protest, he stood, grabbed the tray and started back toward the house. She closed her eyes against the rush of emotion coursing through her.

"You are amazing." The rough sound of his voice made her uneasy. He had stopped in the doorway and turned, balancing the tray on one hand. His eyes traveled the length of her, making her skin pebble.

"You have turned me into something I didn't know I was, Jack. Someone who would play food sex with you in a house where I'm supposed to working. Who'd take all that…that…" She brushed her hair back, sat up more fully and tried to collect her thoughts.

"Six ninety-five," he said, firmly.

"What?" She stared at him.

"That will sell this thing, babe. Six ninety five."

My God. He'd been rocking her world and thinking about what would sell the house?

"Sure, okay, but tell that to my sellers," she declared, snapping back to reality. If he didn't want to acknowledge the earth shattering way he controlled her out in the open in someone else's house, the incredible connection they'd shared, so be it. She could play that game.

"Sorry Sara, I have clients at six thirty tonight. Gotta dash," he threw over his shoulder.

She followed him back into the house, feeling like a complete idiot, furious at him for ruining the moment and nearly blind with humiliation for letting it happen again.

"Sure. So, I guess I'll see you around Jack," she threw at his retreating back. "I mean, next time you need to get off on a Sunday, that is."

He had reached the kitchen by then, put the tray on the counter, and quickly thrown everything back in the grocery bag. She stared at him as he worked. Her body cooled but her brain came to a slow boil.

He turned around to face her as she leaned against the counter trying to control the quaking in her knees. In one short stride, he reached her and took her face in his hands lowering his lips to hers. The gentle nature of his kiss took her by surprise, calmed the rising heat of her anger. His tongue explored, his lips caressed. Finally, he drew back to look deep into her eyes. He grasped her upper arms, and stared into her eyes as if trying to come up with the right words.

"Sara, that was amazing," he kissed her again, lightly. "I'm sorry to rush, but I'll see you soon, I promise you that." He touched her nose. She wondered if he would wash off the smell of her body before meeting his clients. He grinned that million-dollar grin he was famous for, brought his finger to his lips, and gave it a light flick with his tongue.

"I've gotta show five condos to a newly married couple for the next two hours and they won't know where the sex smell is coming from – me, or them." She stared at him from across the kitchen as he finished tidying up and put the tray back where he found it earlier. He grabbed the grocery bag and hooked his arm out in invitation for her to join him on his way out the door.

"See you Jack," she said breezily. "Go on, I should close up here."

She turned away from him, with some effort. Sara's chest tightened when she realized he was actually going to leave without saying anything else to her.

Jesus the man was as bad as everyone said.

Yeah, well what does that make you, Sara?

She glanced at herself in the hallway mirror. Her hair was a mess, her face was red, and her linen shirt hopelessly wrinkled. Holding back tears at her own stupidity, unwilling to register her sense of extreme physical satisfaction, she slammed the house door shut behind her

Once in the car, Jack opened all of the windows and cranked up the radio, letting the Stones drown his agony for the ride home.

Fucking-A. The woman is going to mess you up Gordon. That much was guaranteed.

What he didn't know, for the first time in a long time, was what to do next.

Jack had sincerely hoped that the days away from Sara would have cooled his ardor. Not that he hadn't anticipated a long trip to fun-town with her that afternoon – and had planned and packed accordingly. But he could not get the vision of her standing in the doorway of that fucked up house out of his head now. He hadn't seen a woman look that good in a while, and since he knew full well what her body was capable of – he took a deep breath.

He loved how possessive she got about her listing. It occurred to him that perhaps one of the reasons she held such incredible appeal for him was exactly that – her extreme professionalism. She wasn't doing this job for some extra money while her spouse made the real dough.

Jack shook his head and cranked the music louder before flooring it, letting the powerful car ignite his senses in hopes of clearing his head. He knew that he reverted to discussing the property as a reflex. How many times had he walked into his own friend's houses to play poker or pick them up for golf and automatically start to catalog the problems with the place in his head? He hadn't gotten to his level of earning on one-hundred-percent commission for nothing. And frankly, it helped him stay in control, to keep his body from doing what it wanted before he left, which was to tie her down and fuck her until she was spent, then wrap her up in his arms and kiss her until she begged him for more.

The Stones switched over to classic Clapton. He clenched his jaw. With his level of experience, orgasms for his sex partners were a given. But boredom had set in with the usual manipulations and necessary effort. It had become…what? Mundane? Routine? Well, lucky for him, fate had plopped this female in his path to break that up. She brought out that other side of him. The side that needed to control.

He shuddered, recalling the intensity of her responses. It collided with his need for distance which had caused him to spout out such a stupid lie about having to work tonight. He had felt a reflexive need to move away from her, to protect himself from the feelings he had held down for so long. He had even let his real estate brain take over for a minute; anything to distract him from his bizarre impulse to sweep her into his arms and carry her off into the sunset.

Something in him knew that whatever it was they had could either kill him or make him into something resembling an honest man. The conflict in his head about that threatened him with insanity.

He pulled into his garage beside the SUV he used to cart clients around. Stomping into his kitchen he jumped when his phone buzzed with a text. It was Jason confirming a showing and telling him an offer had come in on a commercial property. Jack threw the phone across the room, noting the satisfactory *whomp* it made against the far wall before he slumped down on his couch, as sights, sounds and smells of Sara tumbled around in his head.

CHAPTER SIX

As the sun baked her skin, Sara sighed and closed her eyes, shifting in her lounge chair. The past week's events ran in a loop behind her eyes, and she winced with a combination of embarrassment and lust.

She'd had an amazing string of successes at work–written three sales agreements and negotiated two others on her own listings. It proved her long standing belief that real estate was a series of Karmic events strung together, testing your resolve, and rewarding the tenacious. On the other hand, her body was on fire since her last encounter with Jack Gordon. She couldn't stop thinking about him, although he'd remained mostly silent ever since their little Open House encounter. It made her antsy and her skin crawl with anticipation and nervous energy that she in turn channeled into work.

She sighed again, and readjusted herself, pissed that the thought of the man made her tingle from head to toe. Damn him anyway. She didn't need him, especially not the drama that seemed to accompany him wherever he went.

Sitting still was not something she had ever excelled at, but Blake and Rob had insisted she join them for the long Fourth of July weekend at their place on Lake Michigan. She really was too busy to take this little break but went anyway. The fact that her brother and his partner knew her much too well made it especially difficult to be around them.

When she would disappear for hours to "sit on the beach" they'd stare, disbelief in their eyes. She knew they would figure it out sooner or later and was not ready for that particular conversation. So, she avoided them as best she could in a seven-hundred square foot lakefront cabin.

She drifted off, the sun and sounds of the Lake Michigan summer afternoon lulling her into sleep. Then she heard him, the low growl of his voice insistent and familiar.

"Sara."

"Hmm…" She crossed her legs.

"Sara, kiss me." The deep voice was insistent.

"No, I can't."

"Yes, you can." The mild lake wind caressed her skin like a lover.

Sara reached her arms up over her head and stretched, as her body reacted to the half-waking dream. Squeezing both eyes shut, she imagined his hands as they moved up her legs, to her hips, across her stomach and to her breasts. Aware on some level that her pussy was dripping wet, her nipples rock hard and if she touched herself right now she'd probably come, she flinched.

"Sara?"

She shook her head, unwilling to respond even in her own head. He was *so* incredibly wrong for her. She knew it. Why couldn't she stop?

"Sara!"

She uncrossed her legs and bent them, to allow the wind to cool her more heated areas.

"Earth to Sara!" She sat up, nearly banging foreheads with her brother.

"Jesus, what?" She frowned at the man who could pass as her twin.

He plopped himself down on the chair and stared at her. She closed her eyes again, determined to ignore him. The last thing she needed right now was an interrogation from an overprotective sibling.

"What is with you anyway?" He grabbed her cheeks in one strong hand and pinched them, pursing her lips just as he used to do when they were kids.

"Get off me," she pulled her face away. Her eyes filled with sudden and alarming tears.

"Nope, sorry, I'm sick of you avoiding me. Since when do you want to sit on the beach, I mean really?" He pushed her over and she half fell onto the sand. Blake's gaze bore into her. He patted the chair in front of him. She sat but avoided any more eye contact, pulled her hair up into a ponytail, and contemplated what in the hell lie she could tell that would convince him to leave her alone. Her phone buzzed. Blake sighed and tried to grab the device before she could reach for it.

"Fuck off, I'm a busy realtor you know, let me work." She held the phone out of his reach over her head, but he was much stronger. Restraining her with one hand on her shoulder, he pressed hard, rendering her immobile as he looked at her phone.

"Ow, damn it," she yelled and watched his face change once he read what flashed on her screen.

"What," she reached for it again.

Blake looked up at her and held the phone out of her reach so she sat back down, defeated. His mouth was set, his eyes hard.

Shit, Jack's just sent another completely inappropriate text like he'd been doing all weekend long.

Blake shook his head, lowered the hand holding her phone and dropped it into her lap. She shrugged. He could have as many opinions as he wanted to about whom she dated. Of course she wasn't exactly "dating" Jack Gordon, her brain helpfully reminded her. She had let him fuck her in two public places with little or no resistance and would have likely let him right there on the beach chair if her wet bikini bottoms were any indication. She wanted him to tell her what to do, when to come, needed to feel his hands on her day and night. Not something she felt comfortable sharing with her brother.

She tucked the phone back in her bag without looking at it. Blake still stared holes into her. He opened his mouth to speak.

"Hey kids," Rob called out. "It's beer-thirty." He joined them and set a tray of drinks and snacks on the large sawed off tree trunk that served as a table between the chairs.

She took the ice-cold glass he handed her. Blake still hadn't spoken or moved from his spot at the foot of her chair so she swung her legs around to sit facing Rob.

"Thanks," she took a sip.

Blake took his beer from the tray and drained half of it.

"Ok, then," Rob said as he settled himself on the chair next to the two of them. "Guess I should have brought you a few more, huh?" He glanced at Sara before he looked at Blake, and they both waited for him to speak.

Sara did not like keeping anything from him. Blake's inflexibility with her these days, his judgmental attitude, made her unhappy to put it mildly. She missed their usual, easy camaraderie. They had hardly ever fought, even as teenagers. A united front in the face of their parent's turbulent relationship had always trumped any sibling conflict. Sara sighed and wiped her sweaty palms on the towel.

"So," Blake stared at her but spoke to Rob. "Your buddy Jack Gordon has taken a shine to my sister."

Rob looked at Sara. She rolled her eyes and shrugged, but her heart fluttered in her chest. Blake had a real knack for making her feel like a naughty high school girl. Fighting the anger rising in her chest, she leveled what she hoped was a neutral expression at him.

"Do you think he's a good choice for her?" Blake continued, as though Sara didn't already know the answer.

Rob contemplated Lake Michigan a moment then turned to Blake and Sara.

"Hard to say," he drained his own beer.

"No, I thought not," Blake stated, avoiding his sister's gaze and ignoring Rob's non-committal response. "But hey, you know, I'm sure he's a lot of fun, eh Sara?" Blake finally looked her way.

His deep green eyes snapped with anger. "I mean that's all that matters to you, right?"

Rob reached over to touch Blake's arm. They had never been much for public displays, so when they did touch, it made Sara glad for her brother's good fortune in the relationship department. But her temper still flared. His bullshit comments couldn't go unanswered.

She started to stand, but Blake held in her place. The three of them sat for a minute like that – connected by the touch of a hand. Rob spoke first.

"Blake, calm down, Sara is a grownup. She can make her own choices." He didn't take his eyes from Blake's face.

Sara pulled her arm out of her brother's grasp.

"Look, I know you mean well," angry tears collected in her eyes. "We can't all be so lucky to find our soul mate you know," she leaned over to Rob who kissed the top of her head. She needed Rob on her side at least a little or she'd never be able to control Blake's increasing overreactions. "Yes, I know him, but we aren't 'together' or anything like that. I mean we work for the same company. We have a difficult transaction going. We're bound to talk…or whatever."

"Um, based on the text I read, I'm willing to guess you guys are doing more than working your deal," Blake looked at her. His eyes had softened, much to her relief.

Her phone buzzed again, rattling her bag. She lifted an eyebrow at her brother and ignored it. Blake ran a hand across his face, put his elbow on one well-toned thigh to prop up his head. Rob patted his leg.

"There, there," he said and smiled his gorgeous, Nordic god smile. "Our Sara is a hottie, after all, and has been without the company of a man for a while. My old friend, Mr. Gordon, is a sucker for that you know."

"Yeah, thanks, that really makes me feel so much better." Blake drained the remainder of his beer. He stood up and took the tray up to the cabin for refills as Sara pulled her phone from the bag. She tried her best not to blush but the message set her nerve endings on high alert.

"Next time I'm going to put one of the creamy strawberries inside your gorgeous pussy and lick you until you purr."

She glanced at the previous message. *"I need to smack that luscious ass again. You game?"* was the prose Blake had read.

She sighed, embarrassed, thrilled, mortified and horny all at once. A state that had been a constant for her since Jack had taken her up against the wall of her office earlier that summer.

Rob put a hand on her shoulder. She looked at him, her face flushed.

"Sara, please, just don't take anything seriously with him," he told her. "I've known him a long time, and witnessed his bullshit first hand. Hell, I helped him perpetuate it on occasion." Blake returned then, bearing fresh drinks for them all. Sara picked hers up and sipped at it, leaning back on her chair. "Just be smart."

"I don't know a thing about him really other than through company gossip," she said, hoping Rob would open up and spill some of Jack's history. Watching the tall, blond Adonis of a man, she had a brief flash of regret that he'd chosen the other team. But her brother had so been unhappy after his last female relationship ended in disaster. He'd told her he was bisexual back in high school when they'd gotten high together during a particularly difficult separation period their parents had endured. Sara had no end of friends madly in love with her handsome, intense, athletic brother. The new wrinkle in his personality hadn't bothered her, other than to make her worry for his ultimate happiness.

When he and Rob had met at a beer festival in Chicago, Blake had fallen hard. While it took a for him to admit it, Rob was persistent, and Sara was truly happy for them both. Their gastro-brewery-pub was one Ann Arbor's hottest eateries right now. They were an amazing team.

"Of course," Rob interrupted her thoughts. "The guy hasn't always had it so easy."

Sara tried not to act too interested. Blake scoffed into his second beer.

"He definitely knows the meaning of hard work. He used to come back every summer and handle construction jobs for his dad's company," Rob motioned for Blake to come sit by him. Sara realized he was trying to humanize the man Blake had demonized. "Talk about a ball breaking bastard," Rob chuckled. "Jack used to dread when he'd get a call from his dad. His mom was a classic Irish princess; alcoholic by the time Jack's sister was in first grade, and dead when Mo was ten and Jack seventeen. You know Keystone Construction," Rob looked at her. "That's Jack's family."

Sara's eyes widened. Blake rolled his.

"Yeah, so Jack partied like a maniac during school but had nearly a four point oh all the way through. His dad wouldn't accept any less and, as much as he hated the old fuck, he wouldn't do anything that might displease him," Rob finished his beer. He sat back tried to pull Blake back against him. Sara smiled. She knew her brother's stubborn streak mirrored hers. He wouldn't melt that easily. Rob shrugged.

"He met Jenna in law school," Rob said, as they both ignored Blake. "What a bitch," he sighed. "Truly, I never got what he saw in her, beyond the obvious fact she was built like a fucking Penthouse pet and smart as a whip," Blake looked over his shoulder at his lover and shifted back in the chair. Rob smiled and put his feet on either side of the chaise so Blake could lean back against him. Rob pulled him close, put his arms around her brother's shoulders and kissed his neck.

"Hey, finish, would ya, before you get all moony on me," she demanded, her heart racing at the thought of getting some real insight into the man who haunted her dreams.

Rob smiled and leaned back, letting Blake fall back against him. "Well, let's say she wins the prize as the one who scored Jack Gordon's whole heart, then stuffed it in a shredder before torching it. The two of them were into some pretty out-there stuff. Had gone to a bunch of BDSM parties. I went with them once." Sara raised her eyebrow at him. "It was some intense shit. It affected Jack in a big way. They'd deemed him a 'natural Master,' whatever the fuck that means. It was like he didn't know if it was a good or bad thing but, Jenna loved it. Wore some kind of crazy necklace thing she called her 'collar' declaring herself Jack's official submissive."

Sara felt her heartbeat in her ears.

"He isn't that bad really," he ran a finger down Blake's neck, across his shoulder and down his arm. "He feels deeply about women, wants to make them happy. He's gotten so good at making them that way on the surface, it's hard to get past that in his own head," Rob insisted when Blake shifted in his seat. "Every single woman he was with – and there were plenty – had his full, complete, undivided attention, until he found the next one. Until Jenna."

Sara finished her second beer and sat up, staring at Rob.

"He called me overseas the week of graduation, told me he'd bought her a ring and was going to ask her to marry him after their law school graduation. He had plenty of money after years being foreman on Keystone job sites." Rob sighed and ran a hand through his thick blond hair. Blake reached up and touched his cheek. "He's my friend, Blake, I'm not gonna pretend otherwise," Rob insisted. "I'm sorry I gave you the wrong impression about him," Blake reached out and took Sara's hand. "He was crazed with something. Some kind of combined buzz over trying to compete at a tough school and taking on this whole-new 'lifestyle' thing she insisted on. It nearly killed him."

She nodded, realizing this was the "ask but don't tell" moment with reference to Jack Gordon.

"Look, I'm not planning on marrying the guy," she told them. "I know him better than most at this point. I know what I'm getting is whatever he's willing to give and it's okay."

Rob grabbed her other hand and pulled her over to sit with him and Blake, putting a strong arm around her.

"I love you, just like I love your brother, Sara, and I don't want you to get hurt. Jack has the potential to be a great guy, but trust me when I say he's yet to fully embrace that right now. Jenna told him she had been fucking both of his roommates for the last six months and laughed at his offer of marriage."

He kissed the top of her head, then Blake's. "You don't live through that, after all the bullshit he had growing up at home, and emerge with your psyche intact. I was in Paris by then at cooking school. One of our old roommates called me to say he'd had to take him to the emergency room during the night. Jack had passed out on their couch, after drinking an entire fifth of bourbon himself. He's been a different man ever since."

Jack chose that moment to buzz her with a text.

Rob touched her shoulder.

"I can't advise you to expect anything more from Jack than what's on the surface. He's spent a lot of years making himself into this guy his is now," he shrugged. "He will either be the worst, or the best thing that will ever happen to you." He put a hand over Blake's mouth before he could speak. "You decide."

Sara looked down at her phone screen.

"Hey, what are you doing? Did you get my messages?"

She sighed and looked over at Rob and Blake. Rob had both arms around her brother's neck, and was kissing his bare shoulder. She lowered her eyes to her phone and responded.

"Yeah. Up North. With brother. He's not happy."

It took a minute before she got her response.

"Blake, right? Partners with Rob Freitag? I know that guy."

"Yep. And he has a pretty definite opinion about you."

"I'll bet he does. He and I did some collateral damage in our day."

"Really? He was into girls?"

"Oh yeah, we were quite the tag team, don't let him tell you any different."

"Wow."

"I'll bet he swings both ways now – some things are hard to give up."

"Hmm. Makes him a good match for my brother. He's done his own fair share of female-related damage."

"Yeah babe, remind me to tell you about your brother's last girlfriend. She's a friend of mine. I wouldn't be surprised if those 2 find a nice young lady to settle down with someday – a nice and cozy threesome. I hear that can work out quite well."

Sara didn't quite know how to respond to that. Thoughts of Jack, in love, vulnerable, hurt...she couldn't process it.

"So what lies are they telling you about me?"

"Well, let's say you are NOT their fav person at the moment."

"Whatev. I get that a lot. So about that strawberry ..."

CHAPTER SEVEN

Nearly two weeks passed before she saw Jack again. He sent daily sexy texts, teasing, inviting but never calling or making any kind of formal invitation to meet. She had to sit on her hands, but she would not allow herself to respond. It somehow energized her, the self-control she had found, in spite of her underlying disappointment with his inability to reconnect.

She had convinced three of her listing clients – including the Open House Picnic one with the view – to lower their prices, and she felt that she'd have offers on two of them soon. Hot yoga had become part of her fitness routine – the perfect exercise for a type-A personality as it included pure physical and mental torture for ninety minutes in a one-hundred-degree room.

The second week of virtual silence after having spent a lonely two hours at her most recent open house, no picnic in sight, she finally admitted feeling absolutely horny. Strange really, having gone so long without close physical contact with a man, how a few highly erotic encounters would leave her with a real taste for more. He probably planned it this way, she thought as she prepped for her weekly sales meeting, realizing that if "he" showed up at that moment, she'd rip his clothes off and fuck him where he stood. The psychological angle of him taking control, making her submit to him, made her shudder with anticipation.

Sara smiled at her reflection in the mirror. If she were completely honest with herself, she'd have to admit that the illicit nature of this thing they were doing, whatever that was, turned her on more than anything she'd ever experienced in her life. She even knew it was likely the entire real estate community knew about them by now. Jack was not known for his silence on the subject of women.

She sighed and brushed her hair back. The occasional twinges of wanting more from him – visions of a future that included him – haunted her, but she would not allow them to gain a foothold. She was an independent woman and successful in her own right. She could cope with a purely physical relationship, as she had claimed to Blake and Rob. But something in her yearned for more. The small taste of his real self, that day at the open house, had not been enough.

Smoothing her hands over the black linen skirt, she turned sideways, admired the sunny yellow top that flared out over the waistband and allowed the slightest hint of cleavage she chosen for today. She allowed herself a small moment of satisfaction. Her latest shoe conquest: a pair of classic patent Jimmy Choos she'd ordered online and had spent an entire commission check to buy, graced her feet. After grabbing her to-go coffee, she headed for the car.

Small talk with Meg and a few other colleagues distracted her on her way into her weekly sales meeting. She took a seat, eating a banana without tasting it.

When she looked up from the latest crisis via email on her phone her eyes clashed with a pair of dark brown ones she didn't recognize across the table. They belonged to a guy looking at her so intently it was a wonder no one noticed. She smiled, and her face got hot when he winked.

The rolled up sleeves of a soft-looking white button-down shirt revealed tanned and muscular forearms. However, instead of looking frumpy and disheveled in his rumpled khakis, he looked, casual, easygoing and…well…hot. Dark blond hair brushed his collar, longer than she usually cared for in a guy, but somehow he made it work. If a central casting call had been for "Sexy California Surfer," he would have the job. She wondered if the European motorcycle she'd seen coming in that morning belonged to him and figured it did. Not usually her type, something compelled her to keep watching him. She blushed when she realized he had raised his eyebrows at her blatant stare, and looked down at her phone as an excuse to ignore him.

"Gang," Pam began. "Allow me to introduce Craig Robinson, our new downtown Stewart Realtor," she nodded at him and he waved a casual hand at the group. "He's spent a few years selling BMW cycles, and brings his A game to our little love nest here. And, if we ask real nice, he just might play the guitar for us. Now, onward – who's got a new listing?"

The meeting proceeded as usual, new listings were described, price reductions announced, "wants and needs" enumerated. Sara ducked her head and tried not to think about her real want or need at that moment, when her phone buzzed with a text.

"Nice skirt. R U dressed underneath in a way that will please me?"

She looked up, wondering how in the hell Jack knew what she had on, all thoughts of the hot new kid across from her forgotten. The phone buzzed again.

"Don't worry. I'll find out myself."

The door to their meeting room flew open and Jack strode in, imposing, impressive, and dressed to kill in a summer-weight brown suit and blue shirt that perfectly matched his eyes. He grinned, raised one hand in a mock formal greeting to them all.

"Jack's here to pitch his new development, and invite us to an opening party, I'm sure." Pam, announced, as she glanced around at the affect his entrance had on her sales staff.

She was a no-nonsense, empathetic, and tough manager, fully in tune with the subtleties and nuances of the highly-strung professionals under her supervision. The older agents who'd been with Jack from the beginning didn't really seem fazed and smiled indulgently as if observing a precocious and slightly naughty four year old. Sara watched the rest of the women straighten up, fidget with hair, their lips, unconsciously drawn by whatever the hell it was he emanated.

The other men in the room watched him, as if studying the technique of a master. Sara fought the urge to lean forward and remained lounged back, coffee cup in one hand and phone in the other. The pheromone level in the room ramped up so high she had to take long deep breaths to keep New Sara at bay.

She glanced over at Craig. He remained cocked back in his chair, ankle crossed over opposite knee, looking straight at her. Her face flushed and she glared at him briefly. He would have no idea who Jack was, of course or why the aura of the room had electrified since he walked in. But he'd learn soon enough. Sara smiled at him, gratified by his blush when she popped a cherry into her mouth and winked.

Jack pitched and walked the perimeter of the room with his slick brochures, describing the latest and greatest mixed-use residential/commercial/retail development that he'd nearly completed on a long-neglected downtown Ann Arbor corner. He'd pause occasionally to touch one or another colleague on the shoulder or bring up some amusing antidote or memory. The female who had his attention would inevitably blush or smack his hand in mock anger.

By the end of his spiel, the room belonged to him, although Sara remained stock-still and had not risen to receive his hand on her shoulder. She looked across the table at Val, one of her closest friends. Jack's wiles had no effect on her whatsoever, as her tastes ran more toward fellow females, but she certainly admired him as a salesman, and Sara was convinced that she knew what was going on between them. Val raised an eyebrow at her. Sara sensed the entire room – including the new guy – observing her, aware of the pornographic movie running through her head that was her Open House from three Sundays before.

With a final flourish and promises of opening party invites to come, Jack headed towards the door, declaring himself on a mission to visit all five Stewart office meetings that morning. He turned at the last minute and locked eyes with her, winked slowly, and his smile morphed into something more than the shit-eating grin of the consummate salesman.

She glared at him. Pam cleared her throat, trying to air the room of the fogginess his little performance had induced and moved on with the meeting, none of which Sara remembered. She struggled to manage her roiling emotions which lurched between elation at his attention, thrill at the fact that her colleagues knew he had singled her out, and sheer, unadulterated arousal, aware of a dampness under her skirt and a hitch in her breath. *Jesus Christ but he was walking testosterone.* And, he knew it, which pissed her off and turned her on in equal measure.

Keeping her emotional distance was becoming tougher with every day that passed. Matching his aloofness took everything she had. She wanted him, needed his voice, touch, lips –and she'd even be willing to cede some of her tightly held control, if he asked again.

She rushed out of the meeting a few minutes early, feigning an emergency phone call, ignoring everyone, including the dark gaze of the new guy. Her closing at noon went well; no last minutes surprises or random craziness from either buyer or seller.

She grabbed a salad and iced tea afterward on the way back to her office. The suffocating heat and humidity seemed more in keeping with a sultry Southern summer than the usually mild and easygoing Michigan climate. Settling at her desk, she returned a call from her most high-maintenance seller:

"Yes, Martha, I agree, but I can't stand at the door of every showing and demand that the buyer's agent leave a card. No, it's not professional but I can't account for the behavior of agents not with my company. Of course, I tell everyone who schedules to leave some sort of card so you know they were there. That's right, we did have a second showing now that you have lowered your price. I'll keep you posted. And please, remember to vacuum the cat hair every day and make sure the air freshener is working. Bye now." She stuck her tongue out at the phone before hanging up.

"Nice save, chick," Val declared over the top of her cubicle wall. "And you must fill me in on that incredibly hot moment you shared this morning with our fine company cocksman," Her grin widened.

Sara rolled her eyes, but knew her skin betrayed her by flushing red.

"Oh, he was just messing with me because I wasn't drooling. Guy can't stand it when he thinks there's a female in the room not completely ready to fall on her knees."

"Hmmm, maybe," Val said, turning to go. "I've known Mr. Gordon a while and I sense something else – anyway, I'm here to listen, when you want to talk."

By three that afternoon, the office buzzed with activity and Sara let work consume her. She talked with prospective clients, provided info for current ones, and was generally sufficiently distracted enough to forget that morning's drama.

As she wrapped up a comparative market analysis for a potential seller, her phone buzzed. Jack. She decided to let him sit for a while. Within five minutes, he had called again. When he called yet again a few minutes later, the phone nearly fell off her desk, buzzing its way across the top.

She grabbed it and hit redial, wondering what was so urgent, and realized the moment he picked up that the appraisal must have hit his desk.

"What the *fuck* is your lender up to?"

Sara winced and held the phone away from her head.

"I haven't seen it yet. Let me pull it up." She searched through her email inbox for the incriminating file.

"Don't bother. I can assure you it won't stand. It's a complete bullshit hack job. We gotta come up with a report to justify a re-do so get your sweet ass over here and help me." He hung up.

Sara sighed, but her body began to betray her when she realized she would be working alongside Jack today, even though he was spitting mad. A low appraisal was every realtor's nightmare and then some. Her buyers needed to borrow a large percentage of the purchase price from the bank. If the bank is told the house isn't worth it, they won't lend.

She punched in a text to him: *"I'll be there in about forty-five minutes."*

"FINE" he yelled via return text. *"I'm on floor until eight anyway."*

She spent about fifteen minutes sprucing up before leaving her office, her brain half-misty with desire and half terrified at the thought of yet another obstacle in the road towards a successful closing of this particular transaction. The drive would have normally taken ten minutes but side street construction gave her an extra twenty minutes to ponder what the evening held.

Sara had done a little online research, claiming to herself it was just to figure out what it all meant. What she found had been a surprising insight into the psychology of people who, like herself, needed to be in control of pretty much all aspects of life, except one how much pleasure could be gained from releasing that very control to someone you trusted.

Trust Jack? Yeah, as if.

But she had, once, and it had provided her with the most incredible sexually charged moment of her life.

Sara squirmed in her seat, remembering how she'd reacted to the pictures and stories. Somehow, the home page of one club in Detroit stuck in her head with its lush colors and vivid yet classy descriptions of the services they offered. One photo in particular of a tall man with dark hair dressed in a suit standing over a woman on her knees with her hands bound behind her, blindfolded, had set her off. She'd had to haul out her trusty vibe to take the edge off after seeing that.

Was that what she wanted from him? To be "topped?" Dominated? Sara had never considered any kink as part of her psyche. But her scary visceral reactions to Jack from the beginning may have an explanation if some of the material she read about this sort of relationship was true. She shook her head. No, that was just crazy. A passing obsession. Jack might be an amazingly dynamic and successful man, but he didn't feel connected to her beyond wanting to mess around. She had to put a stop to it before she fell any deeper.

She entered the original Stewart Realty office with its more traditional perimeter offices, and smiled at the receptionist.

"Hey Sara," the young girl chirped. "Jack's been waiting for you."

She headed towards the back, following the sound of his voice as he argued with someone on the phone and found him at the far corner, in one of the few private rooms. He was leaning back in his large chair, a hand on his face. His voice didn't betray his body's frustration, as he smoothed over trouble.

She leaned in the doorway and observed him before he acknowledged her. The shockingly blue shirt was rumpled, eye-catching tie was off and hanging on the chair back. She found herself focused on his hands – large, talented and the stuff of her dreams during the past few nights. She cleared her throat and he looked up at her. The moment sizzled. She gulped.

Work. She was here to work.

His anger suffused the room. He ended the call, sat back, arms crossed. She remained in the door, keeping her face neutral.

"So, you read this piece of shit, I assume." He indicated the residential appraisal form that declared the value of the house he was selling. The same one he had stolen from her by sleeping with the woman who was selling it, she reminded herself. It stated a value of $220,000. Unfortunately, their contract stated a transfer price of $335,000 – quite the discrepancy.

"Didn't you give the guy your comps?" Comparable sales figures determined the appraised value. Stewart's training demanded that they meet the appraiser at their listing and provide comps themselves to ward off any laziness on the part of the appraisal company.

"No, Sara, I assumed these guys were professionals and could get that info on their own," His tight voice set her nerve endings on high alert. He leaned towards her, his amazing blue eyes bright. "Christ Almighty, he took the most useless sales nearby in spite of everything I gave him. Hell, I practically promised him three hookers and a hotel room." His voice trailed off and he ran his fingers through his hair. She curled her hands into fists against the urge to do the same thing to him. "Fuck. Okay, let's go through this thing and see if we can justify a do-over."

As they worked side-by-side for two hours, Sara's admiration grew as she watched him make calls and cajole honest info out of buyers' agents about various comparable sales. He'd even called homeowners about houses they had purchased from other owners. These "FIZBO's" or "For Sale By Owners," by-passed realtors and would not normally be accepted by appraisers because there was no record of the actual condition of the house in question.

She compiled the data into a ten-page report they would need to provide the lender in order to justify a second appraisal. So absorbed by her task, she had actually forgot the man working alongside her had brought her to repeated, shuddering orgasm not too long ago. She flinched when he touched her shoulder.

"Okay, Jack, I think we have a case." She pulled her hair up and kicked her shoes off under his desk. His extremely tidy and organized workspace gave her pause, and she acknowledged that they definitely did not have that in common. He reached out to touch the iPod in its docking station, filling the room with the sounds of The Foo Fighters.

Figures. He manages to remain hip even on his playlist.

Jack sighed deeply and stretched his arms over his head.

"I fucking hate all appraisers right now, you know?" He declared to the room. "I can't wait until this market reverses itself and they're back to begging us for whatever scraps of business we throw them."

He rubbed his neck. Her skin prickled when he focused back on her. In a heartbeat, he'd grabbed the arms of the chair she was sitting in and rolled her over so that they faced each other. She forced herself to remain calm. But damn if having him so near wasn't rattling every nerve ending she possessed.

"Sorry I went off, baby." He turned her chair around quickly before she could react, so that they sat like passengers on a bus. He rubbed her shoulders as her brain started its usual "resist Jack" mantra. She hated the game he had played with her this morning, hated his easy use of the word "baby" around her, and absolutely despised how much she wanted to hear it again.

She had to get this thing under control.

But maybe you shouldn't? Maybe he should have control.
New Sara crooned in her ear as her body relaxed under Jack's hands.
You read it yourself. Giving over control to another is the first step.
Trusting him to take care of you.

She sighed. That was one thing she could never do. Not in a million years. She barely trusted her own brother and only because she'd had nearly thirty years to learn how to do so.

He leaned in closer to her, his breath on her neck, near her ear. She immediately wished there was no fabric barrier between her skin and his hands.

"You made this easier, no doubt. I think we can make it work." She knew he meant the appraisal but her chest constricted at the thought of making "this" work with him.

"Put those shoes back on." His low, firm voice made something in her give way. "I have been a walking hard on all day since I saw them this morning."

Sara's breath caught in her throat and her nipples contracted as she slipped her feet back into the expensive heels. She tried not to think about the realtors still roaming around the office even though it was almost seven, when most managers and secretaries took off, locking up and leaving the offices available for whatever the workaholic salespeople might cook up.

"Now stand up." His breath heated her skin. She did, and his hands trailed down her body, coming to rest on her hips as he turned her around to face him.

The music segued into some vintage Who, bringing a smile to her face. Of course, the controlling asshole would match her musical tastes. She sighed and looked up at the ceiling, fighting her need for him and her need for distance from him. Gazing at his ruggedly handsome face Sara took a breath as the words "either the best, or the worst thing," flashed across her vision. Her entire body yearned for his. Her desire for his hands on her made her throat close up in panic. They were such a perfect fit on so many levels. But he wasn't here for her. He was here for himself.

He stood, holding her gaze, their bodies grazing, no words between them. Her resolve slipped, but she grabbed it, dragged it back kicking and screaming. Running a finger down his cheek, she relished the feel of his roughened skin. Memories of how perfect his lips felt on hers made her want to fall over. "I should go." The sight of his wicked smile nearly made her come on the spot.

"No," he ran a hand up one arm. "You shouldn't." In the blink of an eye, she found herself pressed against the hard planes of his body.

She shut her eyes against the power of him and his amazing control over her better self. She stood in the circle of his arms, easing back into his dangerous orbit. With a shuddering breath, she looked into his eyes.

"Yes, I should," she shrugged him off and had one foot out in the hallway before he grabbed her arm and yanked her back, slamming the door behind her. His lips shut out her protests, and she melted, hating herself, but allowing newly familiar pleasure light the corners of her brain.

Thanks to the heels, she didn't have to stand on tiptoe to reach his lips as his kiss enveloped her, tugging her down a deep hole of desire. A whirlwind of emotion threatened to bowl her under, bringing her dangerously close to tears.

"Sara," he whispered into her ear. "You are..." he stopped and she stepped away. He took a deep breath. She held hers. His gaze kindled a spark that caught and centered in her core. "Don't leave," he leaned in and kissed her again, his usual urgency absent, the gentle nature of his caresses throwing her off. He broke away, cradling her face with his hands.

She willed him to say more, as Rob's advice about Jack's potential ran through her head again. Intensely erotic memories of his voice, his hands, his lips on her as she let him take control, raced through her rattled head. She laced her fingers at the small of his back and tilted her head, waiting for him finish. Willing him to take control, in spite of herself.

He leaned in to lick the spot between her collarbones.

"I can't give you much right now, Sara," he said against her skin. "But I promise you it won't be boring."

Sara ran her hands up his back, fisted her hands in his coarse black hair and kissed him, kissed him until she saw stars. He moaned into her lips, nearly bringing her to her knees. Rallying everything she had to resist, knowing she deserved more than one more casual fuck from this man, she gripped his upper arms, the crisp cotton of his shirt giving way under her hands.

"I'm sure you won't bore me Jack," she held him at arm's length. "That's not the problem." He stepped away from her, hands on his hips. Sara fought the strange urge to drop to her knees.

"Okay," he ran a hand down his face. "You win."

"I'm not trying to win," she moved another step further away, trying to rally anger or something to resist him. "I'm trying to retain something resembling my sanity."

Jack smiled at her, once again nearly melting what small bit of resolve she had. She stood up straighter. He stepped in closer, cupping her chin in his hand.

"I'm just as afraid of losing mine," he declared, making her skin flush. His lips hovered just out of her reach. "But I'm willing to risk it."

Fully realizing she could be getting the "worst thing" just as easily as the "best thing," Sara succumbed. Jack's lips, tongue, hands, body, she wanted them all, right there, and desire blinded every logical synapse she possessed.

"That's my Sara," she startled at his possessive words. "I know what you need. Let me show you." She nodded as his lips and teeth found her neck, sucked, bit down and made her yelp and moisture flood her panties. The deep growl of his voice, the way he gripped her, it made her weak and shaky, all reactions new to her in the arms of any man.

He reached back and grabbed the beautiful tie he'd been wearing that morning. He raised an eyebrow and without a second thought, she held out her wrists for him. "No, turn around first." She trembled as she turned but he held her steady, pulling both arms behind her.

The soft touch of silkiness grazed her flesh. Jack swaddled her skin in the luxurious fabric, then put his hands on her shoulders and pressed her to the floor. He remained behind her, out of her line of vision. Sara tensed, fighting her body's need.

"This is really why you wanted me here, right Jack? I mean, we could've done this over the phone." Tension she'd held since the awkward morning meeting he'd invaded ebbed away in spite of her submissive position on her knees. She took a breath, let go, and let the touch of his capable hands on her shoulders relax her. The music changed again and Sara heard laughter in the hall, but somehow, she didn't care.

"You like this as much as I do. I can tell. Sort of scary really," he stood in front of her now. She licked her lips at the sight of his bulging zipper. He put a hand on it, making her squirm and her thighs clench. He was suddenly eye level with her, his gaze hard. "I haven't done... this... in a while." He swallowed hard. "But I think it's something I need. And I promise you won't be disappointed." His hand cupped the back of her neck and drew her in. His lips and tongue were fierce, rough and possessive. Sara moaned and leaned into him. She gasped when he broke away.

"Please, Jack. I want you to. I'm," He cut her off by bringing her to her feet then pressing her into the chair. He grinned as he pulled her shaking knees apart. The hand he pressed against her mound nearly burned, bringing a moan to her lips.

"Yes, I know. That's the thing. I know exactly what you want me to do." He slid her skirt up slowly, hooked a finger in her panties and with a jerk, had them ripped in two. "Don't ever wear these again." She nodded and leaned back as his lips settled around her clit, tugging it into his mouth, and tried very hard not to scream.

"Ask me." His voice was low. She shuddered. "Ask me if you can come."

The room faded. There was only her and the man between her knees. No anger, no stress, no residual discomfort. Only him.

"May I...oh God," She gripped her hands together, still bound in the tie, as he teased her with his tongue. "Please, may I come? Jack?"

"Yes. You may." He pressed fingers high inside and sucked her clit back between his lips. The orgasm ripped through her, tearing her in two as effectively as the discarded silk on the floor.

Jack smiled against Sara's skin, ran his tongue down her pussy lips, dipped into her pulsing center and reveled in the smell and sight of her pink, silky perfection. The sound of her trying not to yell made his cock swell harder. He had forgotten how much he loved this.

He'd always excelled at taking charge, whether at work, on the golf course, a building site, anywhere. People looked to him to do it. He'd been captain of three varsity sports teams in high school and president of his fraternity for two years in college. It seemed natural to fall into a roll of formal Master with his sex partners. But something about it had a dark hard edge that he avoided. It brought something out in him he didn't think he liked. After going full bore with Jenna for so long only to have her jump into a three way with his roommates without his permission, without even telling him – he'd doubted himself ever since.

He nuzzled Sara's pussy once more, his brain buzzing with energy, knowing he'd made a connection with her that wouldn't be denied. But, did he want it? He stood, watching her, one hand on his straining zipper, the other wiping his lips. Her amazing green eyes sparkled, as the post orgasm look he loved stole over her face.

The room darkened. "Stand up." She rose to her feet. "My turn." He pressed her to her knees again, groaning at the sight of her shoes, her face. Dear God, everything about the woman flipped every erotic switch he possessed, including the one he thought he'd taped over with an "out of order" sign. The one labeled: Master. The whole scene made him feel powerful, content, and potentially dangerous. He unzipped and released his already weeping cock to her lips.

She ran her tongue around the edges, slipped it into the slit pearled with his fluid. Thighs trembling he fisted his hands in her silky hair. "All the way down Sara. I need you to." She looked up and locked eyes with him before slipping her beautiful mouth over him.

He sucked in a breath, felt his head hit the back of her throat as she relaxed and swallowed him. He eased out, then back in, his brain shutting down and his body taking over. He could handle this. He…

"Oh fuck," he shoved his hips forward, braced one hand on the wall and let go. Let himself fall. "Swallow it Sara. I'm gonna come." His voice whispered, but the rush of orgasm roared in his ears, blinding his vision. He'd forgotten how intense he climaxed when in this mode. "Oh dear God..." He grunted, thrust down her throat once more and released as the room narrowed, went black, then cleared.

Sara had never been a huge fan of giving head. Didn't even think she did it that well. But when Jack had released his thick cock in front of her eyes, no force on the planet could have kept her from it. She wanted it in her mouth, down her throat, so badly she could barely see.

He tasted salty, musky, and delicious. The sensation of his hands in her hair, the way his hips angled up and his legs spread to keep steady made her pussy twitch. Her clit swelled, pulsed and her already wet thighs slickened further as she swallowed him.

Her man. She was pleasing her man and the concept of that when he grunted and exploded down her throat made her pussy spasm and release, as she groaned around his girth. He kept thrusting, tugged at her hair bringing that edge of pain to her pleasure, as his fluid dripped down her chin. When he stilled he immediately reached down to pull her up and into his arms, releasing her wrists so she could wind her body around him.

Dear God you have it bad. And for Jack Gordon no less.

Jack's kisses had an economy of energy about them – he didn't waste time trying to pull her entire mouth into his. He licked her lips, as his breathing evened out. He waited for her to want more and, when she grabbed the back of his neck and pulled him closer, he sighed and wrapped his hands up in her hair. He broke away and moved his lips down her neck, nuzzling and biting into her flesh. He stroked her legs, moving closer up under her skirt to her ass. When he cupped her there, caressing and squeezing, he returned his mouth's attention to hers.

Oh my God, his lips. Desire intoxicated her when she realized this was the longest time they'd spent on a kiss in all of their encounters. Forcing all logic deep down under a need that kept roaring in her ears, Sara sighed

"You do something to me Sara." His voice was low, raspy. "I don't get it. I don't even know if I like it. But I can't get enough of it."

She felt so alive, so incredibly sexy in these shoes, in the arms of this man desired by so many. His words only reinforced it.

"My God, I think I could fuck you in those shoes all night."

Sara stepped out of his arms, smoothed her skirt down, using some tissue in a box on his desk to clean up. She faced him, not sure what to say. Her heart raced, her mind spun.

Why couldn't they keep their hands off each other anyway? He was so irresistible. But so wrong.

He sat, seemingly dazed and grinned up at her, tie draped back around his neck. Glancing at the clock Sara realized it was nearly eight o'clock and the office should have emptied out. What now? Should they eat together? Snuggle on a couch? Watch a movie? Or part ways and meet up again next time he was horny?

New Sara was sated, but something else tugged at her subconscious. A need to flee his presence, but at the same time wanting to crawl up into his lap and be petted like a housecat. The two impulses warred, making her dizzy and angry. She had a moment of pure panic, but Jack sat back in his chair, and tugged her into his lap, kissed her neck and held her close.

"Relax baby," he muttered into her ear. "Like I said – I can promise fun. No need to get worked up." he grinned at her and Sara's inner alarm clanged. "So, is it a Mexican food night again?"

She arranged her face into a frown, coming up with excuses to escape.

"I suppose, but I'm going to yoga at six tomorrow so I wanted to be home early."

"Yeah, you like the sweaty hour and a half of torture?" he ran a finger down her cheek, jaw, neck.

"No, but I can already see the benefits, so I'm gonna keep going." She moved away from him, sat down in his other chair.

She needed something from him she and knew damn good and well he'd never give her. He could play at controlling, dominating, being the master of her body but the Jack Gordon that she knew did not make emotional connections with women, only physical ones. She realized she should get far away from there before she sunk any deeper. All her own brave talk about merely wanting the base connection with him she'd thrown at her brother was lost in a haze of desire for something more – something she swore she'd never, ever expect from a man.

He stared at her, confusion evident in his face.

"What? Let's go, I'm starving. I haven't eaten since the fruit bowl this morning."

"You know what, Jack; I'm going to pass on the afterglow dinner." She reached down to adjust her shoes, gathering her Old Sara together to resist the temptation to drag out their "date."

"Um, okay, that's cool."

Damn. Stop looking at me like that or I will let you fuck me again, I don't care who watches.

The words "Don't expect more from Jack than what's on the surface," careened around in her head. Her heartbeat refused to slow. This was her chance. She should take it. Tell him how she really felt. Tell him... what? A familiar panic rose in her throat.

Why can't it be simple? Why can't you open your mouth and speak?

But her need for space overwhelmed her desire to go anywhere else with him.

"You sure? I wanted to try out this new place with you, my little hot pepper lover."

It was her turn to grin.

"Yep, but thanks anyway," she grasped the tie that he now had draped around his neck, pulled his mouth to hers for a tantalizing final kiss. She broke it off, turned on her heel, and exited, not looking around to see who was watching.

Waving at the remaining agents gathered around a computer, Sara breezed out the door, only barely resisting the extreme temptation to turn around and race back to him. While Old

Sara congratulated her on her resolve, both Saras missed the rare look of disappointment and frustration that crossed Jack's face as he watched her leave.

Jack braced himself against the doorjamb and watched her sashay out, his heartbeat still ringing in his ears from that monster climax. Passing a hand over his face, he eased back inside and shut the door. The room held the essence of their lust, and he took in a deep breath of it, wanting to hold it in his memory banks. One word surged through his brain: mistake.

Huge, colossal error in judgment. He never should have done it. She wasn't ready. Hell, he wasn't ready. He obviously was no fucking good at it anymore if he couldn't even get her to stick around after they'd gotten off. He wanted to talk, to feed her dinner with his own fingers, to take her home with him.

Damn the woman.

He stood, stretched and relished the deep relaxation in his back and hips that only a truly gargantuan orgasm can offer. Every deal was important to Jack, and he sensed the same thing about Sara. When that piece of shit appraisal had hit his inbox, he couldn't resist a little thrill of excitement, knowing they would have to work together to fix the potentially colossal problem.

He had tried to tamp down his rising desire at having her in his personal space again, focusing on the task. But when he smelled her perfume the minute she walked into his building, he knew he was a goner. He wanted more than anything to see that well-fucked face again, and decided he was going to make it happen.

He had forced himself to stay away from Sara since their little picnic. The scary sense of falling down a dark hole, of losing control, of letting go and giving in to her completely was something he couldn't face.

So, he dealt with it in the way he'd adopted in years past. Push it away, far away, and stay the hell away from the woman causing it. He'd spent a boring Fourth of July with a few buddies up at Torch Lake, fishing, drinking, and poker – a regular sausage fest. Usually time with his friends set him straight. Two were still married and constantly moaning about their wives, one was divorced but with a new girlfriend no one liked. Jack was their torchbearer. The guy they lived vicariously through. But the weekend did not have the desired effect on him at all.

He had spent most of the time composing his next text to Sara, relishing their sexy contact via the phone. He loved controlling her that way, but knew it was as much for his benefit as hers. He wanted to picture her going about her business, but ready for him. Actually, it was all he did lately, which pissed him off and made him want her more. He was a walking, talking hard on the entire time, relief only coming in the shower or first thing in the morning, thanks to his good friend Lefty left hand. He took endless ribbing from his buddies, but would emerge from his room or the bathroom and flip them off before grabbing another beer.

"Knocking the edge a bit more than usual, eh Gordon?"

"Jesus, I gotta see this girl Jack, wanna share?" The general nature of the comment from the peanut gallery did nothing but aggravate him.

But with her in his office, it had taken all he had to not sweep her up in his arms, to hold her tight, beg her to go home with him. He could not for the life of him figure out why he didn't, but the look on her face had forced him to remain nonchalant. That look – skeptical, cynical, somehow reading him for his usual shallow prick persona – it stopped him cold. He had no one but himself to blame.

He should never have gone there with her. That part of him – the part that got bone shattering release from being on top, from mastering a woman, body and soul – it was dead; killed in the flash of realization all those years ago, in the hard depths of one woman's eyes, the sound of her laughter. As he made his way to his car, the smell of Sara on his skin, memory of her sweet pussy tilted up to him, of her offering body to his control, caused his cock to stir under his trousers.

Christ, I haven't been this constantly horny since I was senior in high school.

All he had in his head on the drive home was the gut-deep need for Sara. He wanted her, in his life, in his bed. He was counting the days until he could get inside, truly inside, her again.

CHAPTER EIGHT

The computer screen she'd been staring at for an hour blurred in front of Sara's eyes. Rubbing one with the heel of her hand, she stood, giving up in disgust. The cute new guy, Craig, had been helping her with a presentation, using listing information straight from the computerized multi-list system employed by realtors to find and search the housing market for data. But it had hit a glitch and wouldn't let her download for some reason which had set her back nearly an hour on a hot Friday afternoon.

As the agent "on floor," Craig was called to the front to meet a potential client who'd wandered in off the street. The Stewart Realty downtown office was designed as sort of a decoy. From the street, it was set up to look like a small coffee shop, with an art gallery, occasional live music and classy, comfortable seating options scattered around the front room.

The high ceilings were exposed to the rafters with very expensive lighting made to look haphazard and casual. The actual offices remained hidden in the back, behind the receptionist's desk. Up front, flat screen TV's stayed tuned to either news or sports, but smaller screens, visible from the sidewalk on a very busy downtown street, displayed professional listing videos. People were curious at first, but now that they understood it, the office got all sorts of foot traffic, as people were encouraged to bring in their sack lunches and to open laptops in the space. The carefully selected realtors who populated the office were consummate, yet understated, sales people, knowing when to sit and chat and when to leave people alone.

It was a groundbreaking concept in an age when more and more real estate offices were "virtual." Aside from actually showing houses, most of the work could be done on a laptop creating reports, or on a smartphone setting appointments. At a time when most buyers found their realtor at a random open house or by sending an inquiry email from a listing on the main realty website, finding ways to connect personally remained tough. So, why not create a place that the Stewarts knew would be a loss leader at first, but be somewhere potential clients would come to associate with ultra-professional sales people? A relaxed and inviting atmosphere they could even rent out for private parties; not designed to generate a profit for about six or seven years but become a would be, well-established Ann Arbor entity.

The very attractive receptionist was also a licensed realtor who knew when to hit the buzzer under her desk to summon the agent on call or when to let the people wander, sit, drink the free coffee or filtered water and leave them alone. It worked. After four and a half years, it had become one the top-producing offices in the formidable Stewart Realty Empire. An inordinate amount of luxury and super-luxury homes got listed and sold by the agents within it and Sara was no exception. The report she had been trying to generate would garner a listing the potential sellers had valued at two-point-five million, but thanks to the data she was trying to pull, Sara was struggling to justify a price just over half of that amount.

As she rounded the corner and ran her hand down the wall where Jack had taken her that first night, Sara's scalp prickled. She frowned, angry at the constricted feeling in her chest when she pictured his compelling face, inky black hair and deep blue eyes. Shaking her head to stop his image from rattling around inside her skull she turned the corner as Chris, the receptionist, headed the other way. The two women laughed when they nearly collided, and Sara couldn't help but notice the admiring eyes of the young girl as she looked at Sara. Everybody must know about her and Jack. There was no way to keep secrets in their small community. And Jack had a big goddamned mouth, Sara knew, so likely had bragged far and wide about fucking her in the hallway, at the open house, and in his office.

"Hey, Sara, can you come help Craig," the young woman asked. "He's about to sustain claw marks out here."

"Sure, but what can I do?" She peeked around the corner. Spying the young blond man who had every female in the office swooning seated next to an attractive older woman on one of the couches, she started to turn back and tell Chris that Craig could handle himself and needed to learn how to use his amazing good looks to his advantage. When she saw the woman place a hand on Craig's navy blue clad thigh. She saw him flinch and look straight at her, his eyes pleading for help.

She stifled a giggle as Chris pushed her into the room. Craig stood, his knees hitting the table in front of him as the woman in the dark designer jeans and tight polo shirt that highlighted her ultra-toned form kept her eyes glued to his ass.

"Darling," he declared, holding out a hand for Sara and motioning with his head for her to come closer. She smiled and played along, taking his hand, letting him pull her close to his body, tucking her under his arm.

"Carolyn, may I introduce you to my partner," he leaned down and planted a kiss on Sara's lips. "In real estate and now," he kissed her again. "In life."

Sara glared into his deep brown eyes, but went along with the show. She turned to Carolyn, and put both arms around Craig's slim hips, resting her head on his shoulder before releasing him and shaking the woman's hand.

"So pleased to meet you Carolyn," she purred. "How can we help you?"

The two of them giggled like a couple of middle school kids after waving at the woman's retreating back. She'd signed a listing agreement with them for her million-dollar marital home in order to downsize into a three-quarters of a million dollar downtown condo. Craig pulled Sara in close, holding her, murmuring into her hair.

"You are amazing."

Sara remained in the circle of his arms a minute longer before pulling away.

"Yeah, gee, darling," she held his arms and stared at him. "Nice one."

He shrugged and brushed his too-long blonde hair from his forehead.

"Well, it was either get engaged to you, or let her rape me in the broom closet," he admitted. Sara loved that he actually colored a little at that.

Damn he was adorable.

"I like my choice," he said, his voice soft, still looking into her eyes.

"So," Sara broke the moment before she let herself get caught up. "Now that you have put "plan a wedding" on my to-do list, can we please get back to my presentation dilemma," she gestured to the back of the building. Craig opened the door for her leading to their work area. "You should know," he said following her back. "I have a ton of nephews and a niece and they will all want to be in the wedding." Craig leaned on her cubicle entrance as she sat, trying to calm her breathing. She had work to do, and noticed she'd missed two calls and three texts. Mr. Office Popularity needed to leave her to it. She leaned back in her chair, crossing her legs while giving him a pained look.

"Well you should know I have to figure out a way to have my brother be maid of honor," she stated. "And he hates kids so keep them away from him."

She spun back around and faced her computer screen, loving the sound of his laughter and the friendly hand he placed on her shoulder. When he rolled his chair closer so he could study the screen with her, she caught a whiff of something on him, underneath the subtle scene of cologne. Unable to place it she flinched as he leaned in to punch a few keys, bringing up exactly the information she needed. His arm brushed her breasts, but she let it go.

"Wow." She stared at the screen now populated with the data and charts she had been struggling for an hour to create. Craig leaned back, his long arms behind his head. Sara drank in the sight of his wrinkled button down, navy blue trousers, blonde hair falling over one eye. Her heart sped back up.

"Yeah, I rock," he said, never taking his eyes from hers. Sara knew at that moment if he had reached out for her, she would have kissed him. An odd feeling. Not like the raw chemical response that Jack's presence elicited. More like a comfortable moment when you suddenly decide an old friend would make a great lover. Craig merely sat, observing her, not coming any closer. Sara broke the connection when something occurred to her that she'd been meaning to ask him.

"How does an adorable Southern boy like you end up in our little Midwestern paradise anyways?"

Craig crossed his legs knee to ankle. Sara tried very hard not to observe how it stretched the fabric of his wrinkled trousers over his crotch.

"Oh, you know, the usual, father takes a promotion with large automotive company, moves family consisting of one angry seventeen year old boy because all of the other sons are in college," he looked up at the ceiling. Sara stayed quiet.

"After I graduated he had a massive heart attack. Dead before he hit the floor, apparently," Sara put a hand over her mouth but Craig sat up, the look in his eyes somehow precluding any sympathetic commentary.

"So, I stuck around here to help my mom, because all my brothers had lives involving other people. But I dropped out of school. I found a band to play in, sold motorcycles a while, got my real estate license, enrolled in some classes at the U and hopefully next year can get back to school full time…maybe…haven't decided yet really," he grinned, reminding Sara how very adorable he was. Her brain did a quick calculation.

"How old are you anyway?"

Craig raised one eyebrow. "Old enough to drink."

"Well, thank God for that. Wouldn't want anyone to take me for a cougar. Now, about this wedding…"

A clatter of activity in the main hallway broke the moment. Several of their male colleagues walked by.

"Hey Sara, Craig," Rick called out. Sara winced. She'd actually gone out with him once. He'd been all over her from the beginning of their date like a damn octopus.

"Yo, Taylor," a voice called out. "You win that golf outing last night?"

"Nah," Rick stopped to the left of her cubicle opening. "That bastard Gordon swooped in at the last minute and snagged it."

Sara looked up at the mention of Jack's name, aware of Craig's intense stare.

The two men stood sipping their coffee beyond where Sara and Craig sat.

"Jesus, did you see that chick on his arm?"

"Yeah, what else is new? Gordon has the best tux, gets the best prices on the auction shit, and has a frigging super model for a date." She shut her eyes. The other man laughed. Both were successful, as was required of this highly visible office and neither a slouch in the looks department. But Jack Gordon operated on a completely different plane. Having spent a few years building a successful law practice, he'd seemingly pitched it all in to go "where the money was" selling real estate. Proficient in all aspects, including high-end commercial and with a builder's license to boot, he had been their top seller for nearly ten years, and sold almost five-hundred-million dollars' worth of land, houses, offices and retail space last year alone.

"Yeah, that fucker," the other man said, clapping his colleague on the back. "He was pretty lit by the end though, she was sort of holding him up, didn't look too happy about it either."

"Well the guy never turns it off, you know?"

"Yep, the phone was never out of his hand. I saw him at one point in the hallway back towards the head, leaning on the wall, and told him his date was looking for him. He shushed me up, like he was hiding from her."

Sara gritted her teeth remembering the series of explicit sex texts she'd exchanged with the man in question last night. She laced her fingers together and held them tight. As if sensing her distress in some cosmic universe, Jack sent her a text then, causing her phone to rattle across her desk. She looked at it, then for some reason up at Craig, who shrugged his shoulders and walked out of her cubicle. Sara watched as her phone buzzed its way onto the floor.

By the end of the day, she had worked herself into a frenzy of anxiety and distress. The man was nearly as good at making himself scarce as he was at showing up at inopportune moments. While New Sara yearned for his eyes, lips and hands, she kept rallying her inner Old Sara to remind herself that he was an egocentric, womanizing asshole and her brother was right. She owed it to herself to get as far as possible from him, stop all this nonsense; it was messing with her head. He could not be the answer. No matter the tiny voice that kept insisting that he might be, if she'd let him.

He had certainly proven to be a valuable adviser lately with her more difficult transactions. She'd find herself faced with some dilemma and would automatically text or call Jack to get his perspective. The fact that she hadn't given him any indication she wanted anything from him beyond his body and so had no place to complain drifted through her thoughts. He would offer advice, a laugh, top it with a pornographic suggestion or two then sign off.

It took two to communicate. She knew and they were getting to be experts at dancing around emotion and cutting right to the real estate...or the physical. Sara was even getting used to the constant ache in her gut when she went longer than a couple of days without any contact with him. Now, knowing he had been with some "supermodel" of a woman last night... she clenched her eyes shut at the desk.

Oh crap, Sara, get a grip. He doesn't owe you anything. You don't know what you want anyway. How is that fair to him? Maybe you should focus on that instead.

She rushed out of the office and made it home by six. Changing into running gear and strapping her iPod to her arm felt like positive steps. Taking action to drown out the constant low-grade buzz of wonder about what Jack was doing right then and with whom. The comforting strains of her warm-up reggae filled her ears. She dashed down the steps and stretched her hamstrings on the small front lawn, bending at the waist, legs spread wide. The realization that she was not alone as she slowly stood didn't really surprise her. It seemed perfectly natural to meet Jack's eyes as he hopped out of his car, dressed for exercise, his smile wide at the sight of her ass up in the air.

"Done with your sissy stretching yet?" He smacked her rear before taking off down the sidewalk. As she rolled her eyes and began to follow him, Sara let herself be pissed all over again at him for invading the one area of her life where she could be alone, pushing her body, forcing herself to go further. She would not let him turn this into some sort of race. But the natural competitor in her got revved at the sight of him, far out in front.

On his heels for the first two miles, the soundtrack of her favorite heavy rock music pounding in her ears propelled her faster. Sara met and conquered the wall she always hit at three miles and overtook him. The humid August evening held a hint of fall. The sweat poured off her but she felt strong – and utterly beyond caring where Jack was.

As she turned a corner, headed back west and around the local high school campus Sara sensed Jack's presence very near. She heard his breathing which seemed annoyingly calm for a guy who'd semi-sprinted for a couple of miles behind her. The thought broke her concentration and her stride, and he overtook her.

He touched her shoulder as they approached Pioneer Woods, the area of the campus that was wooded and hilly, with cross-country trails threaded through it. She slowed and followed him as he crossed the fields onto the trails. They were near her six-mile mental barrier and still had to get back home. Traipsing around on cross-country paths didn't sound like a good plan.

But, she would not let him beat her, not at this. He seemed at ease with his body's running rhythm, a mere sheen of sweat across his brow, as if he could carry on for a marathon's length. The indie rock music blaring in her ears provided her a bit of extra boost so she matched his pace and entered the cool shaded forest.

She'd run the very same paths during her four years of cross-country practices. After completing the first mile and a half, he started slowing. She drafted him, grateful for the respite. Her heart pounded and her legs already wobbled.

Jack glanced back, slowed more and then stopped, which made her run right past him. She slowed, her breathing labored, arms flapping then turned. Jack stood in the middle of the path, hands on hips, chest heaving with exertion. Sara tried to square her reaction to his sudden halt and her own body's adrenaline rush from the punishing run and his amazing physical presence. Without preamble, Jack crossed the few feet between them, reached out and yanked her close, his mouth on hers. The kiss spoke volumes – punishing and intoxicating.

He walked her backwards, still kissing her, pushing her off the trail. Sara tasted salt, tried not to collapse in his arms. When she started to remove the ear buds from her ears, he stopped her.

"No," he motioned for her to keep them in and let the music play.

He reached around and grabbed her ass, pulled her against his body. Their tongues tangled, and Sara heated up, familiar zinging sensations shot through her as Jack possessed her with his mouth. His aggression acted as an extreme aphrodisiac, and she met him halfway, fisting her hands in his damp hair.

Jack worked them into a semi-secluded glen off the main trail and propped himself up against a giant tree trunk. His wicked smile nearly undid her as he released her hair from its holder, burying his hands in it, making her tilt her head back.

Jack grasped the exposed skin of her neck with his lips and teeth, forced a thigh between her legs. Licking sweat, biting down on her jugular, tugging on her hair, he seemed to find every trigger she had by intuition.

She gasped when he picked her up, wrapped both legs around his waist, and pressed against his erection, let her visceral need for him take over. The music pounded in her ears, while his hands and mouth roamed all over her. She started to move against him, pressing her needy flesh against the rock hard cock still confined by his shorts. She shut her brain down before it warned her about making out in public with him again. Her eyes popped open. Jack's sapphire blues sparkled, dark with lust.

This is absolutely crazy.

She forced herself to slide down his body. He turned them, leaned her against a large tree, one with a notch between two trunks, which allowed her to keep her clit pressed against his upper thigh. He shoved her sports bra up, and rolled a rock hard nipple between his fingers, making her groan, closing off the clamor of warning taking hold in her brain.

His lips reached hers again, his tongue probed in and out, in an unmistakable rhythm. He shoved his leg farther between hers, giving her the contact she needed. She shuddered as her engorged clit rubbed against his hard thigh, faster and faster.

"Don't come yet Sara. You know the rules." That voice, low, commanding and sure, made her shudder. "I'll tell you when."

She gasped as he shoved some combination of fingers inside her, reaching up high, letting his thumb press against her clit. He teased, pulling out then back in, fucking her, as he sucked one nipple then the other to hard, sensitive points. Sara thought if she could see herself right now, her skin would be glowing. When he had her, had his hands and lips on her, forcing pure energy through her nerve endings, it proved breathtaking, and addictive. "Oh Jack, Please." She fisted her hands in his damp hair, shoved her hips against his hand. "May I?" He grinned up at her, licked his lips and covered her mouth and her pleas for release.

The small, whimpering noise she made down in her throat nearly made Jack insane with lust. The smell of heat, sweat, and her delicious body swirled around him. Her pussy clutched at his fingers, pulsing, just on the edge as he stretched in further, knowing exactly where to touch her already. Teasing with his lips he shoved her harder against the tree trunk.

"Take my cock out." He growled. "Rub it. Fast and hard, like you want to." He leaned down to lick the sweat rolling down her long neck. "Then I'll let you."

The touch of her hand made him groan and press higher, stroking that magic spot. He bit down on the salty delicious flesh of her shoulder and muttered. "Come now baby. Come now." She obliged, in a delicious gush of fluid, calling his name, her hips jerking against his hand, which sent him straight over the edge. His vision darkened and he grunted and coated her stomach as she clutched him close, tugging his hair pulling his lips to hers.

He made his own whimper when their lips met, when her tongue thrust into his mouth, making that final connection he'd grown to love. He pulled his fingers from her body, and she released him, leaning back against the tree. Reaching out to use his shirttail to wipe her hand, she smiled.

"Tell me something Jack." He nodded, hands on his hips, trying to wrap his head around what had just happened. He was a premeditated sort of guy - liked to plan his encounters. And she'd pulled him into not one, not two, but three utterly unplanned sex acts that were among the hottest in his memory. She made him so eager to get her alone, with nothing but them, a flogger and restraints he could fairly taste it. "What is all of this anyway?" He stared at her. An unfamiliar anger rose in her eyes.

"Um, what is all of what?" He knew what she meant, but couldn't answer it because he had no answer. The very images flashing through his fuzzy brain – of her tied down, at his mercy, screaming his name as he brought her to glorious climax again and again before being able to sink deep inside her with his cock and not just his fingers and tongue – represented something utterly impossible. He couldn't do it to her. Or to himself. The connection would mean too much and he honestly doubted his ability to handle it.

He settled his face into what he hoped was neutrality. "All a lot of fun, best I can tell, babe." He patted her ass and jogged off wincing at his own lameness.

What now Gordon? Seriously, you'd better get this whole thing under control, and not just the playtime. She needs some breaking down. You know you can do it.

When she flew past him, he picked up speed, dreading the nearly six miles back to her house, as his body went into post-climax shut down mode.

Determined with a stubbornness born of self-preservation, Sara put her hands on his shoulders went up on tiptoes and gave him a peck on his kiss-swollen lips. She'd spent the entire run back coming up with excuses to get him to stay, to take her inside and fuck her silly, take a nap then start all over again. Dear God she had it bad. But, when they jogged to a stop in front of her condo, he stood and stared at her.

After glancing around with what seemed like nervousness, he put his hands on her hips and pushed her away. "I have to go." Not sure if she was shocked or not, she watched him open his car door and get behind the wheel.

"What, no good-bye kiss?" She propped her arms on the door when he rolled the window down and motioned her over. Her heart pounded with disappointment and anger. She really wanted to believe he'd say something about grabbing a shower and picking her up later for dinner, or a movie, or something. Instead, he cupped her face with one hand, and kissed her with a surprising tenderness.

"You continue to amaze me Sara." His voice was low. "But I'll catch you tomorrow – it's poker night at my house and I, ah, I still gotta buy beer."

She frowned, stood and watched as he drove away, her body cooling down in more ways than one. Heading inside with a sigh, the recognition that she was ready to agree to anything to stay near him, but apparently he'd had his fill and could go on his merry way, drew a string of curses from her lips. She stood in the shower, post-run and post-orgasm adrenaline still coursing through her system. The lack of him, the empty space where she wanted him to be right now made her chest ache.

Please, Sara, get a grip and do not think you are in love.

She let the water sluice over her flushed face. She had a ton of work still tonight. The thought of her to-do list forced Jack to the back of her brain as she scrubbed and emerged, determined to treat today's little encounter casually, like he undoubtedly was. Staring at herself in the bathroom mirror, her body red from the hot water and earlier physical exertion, Sara suppressed the panic rising in her throat.

They were too much alike, both avoiding anything that hinted at an emotional connection. She sighed. Why she couldn't just own up to it and tell him how she felt, it was beyond her. The tension had ramped up to a scary level, but the conflict in her heart wouldn't let go. She stomped out to the living room, grabbed a water bottle, and fired up her laptop. The websites she'd visited were still on the screen.

"The Suite," the BDSM club downtown that had mesmerized and educated her was front and center. She stared at the photo again; the one that made her skin pebble and her brain buzz with need.

Damn him.

She gritted her teeth. She did not want this.

Or did she?

CHAPTER NINE

Jack gunned his engine. He had shocked himself, really, coming up with yet another line of bullshit so quickly. God, he wanted her – more and more every day it seemed. But she kept him at arm's length, making him doubt his every move, his very need to control her.

You could change that you know, you idiot.

The Corvette's engine rumbled and the power under his hands gave him a familiar comfort.

Open your stupid mouth and tell her how you really feel.

He had to grip the steering wheel hard to resist turning around and driving back to her. His phone buzzed with a text and he smiled, anticipating Sara's request to return. Instead, the screen showed Jason's message about some random work related crap. He sighed, and made the turn onto his tree-lined street.

Jack realized what was happening. Her strength drew him – her absolute independence turned him on and made him need to prove to her that she didn't have to be so damned strong. He desperately needed her to want more from him, and for the first time in his vast experience, had no idea if she even gave him a second thought every time they'd messed around.

Well, hell, no wonder you don't think you can handle being a Dom again. You can't even get a handle on the woman you want as a sub. Jesus.

After that first night in the office hallway he'd been single minded as all the old shit tumbled around in his head. Obsessing over a woman was not new but he recognized the difference this time. The aura of complete and utter control over another person's soul, their happiness and satisfaction and all the trappings – bondage, spanking, orgasm denial – he fucking missed it. Something about Sara brought it all roaring back with a vengeance. He smacked the steering wheel.

After that incredible moment in the trees, he'd experienced a surge of pure panic. The admission in his own head that he could easily scoop her up and carry her over his back Fred Flintstone style, never letting her out of his sight, forced him to make up some stupid lie to escape and retreat. Usually he couldn't wait to get away from whatever female he'd had. Now, in some perverse reversal of logic, he reverted to silly lies about "plans already made" to keep from acting on his impulse to stay, to never leave her side.

Way to blow it John Patrick. Poker night for God's sake – where did that come from? Now what?

Jack threw his keys on the kitchen counter and splashed cold water onto his face. He leaned on his hands and gazed out of the window at the patio he'd had installed last spring. Designer furniture graced every corner, a two-thousand-dollar grill sat perched near the edge, all the shit that had made him completely happy a few months ago, mocked him now with their shallowness.

"Fuck!" He ran upstairs to the luxurious master suite he'd designed and built himself. He loved his thirties-era bungalow in one of Ann Arbor's premiere neighborhoods, had spent hours converting it into a glorious home to his exact specifications. The steam shower enveloped him, soothing his frazzled nerve endings as he leaned both hands on the imported Italian tile walls, letting the water run down his neck and across his shoulders. When he closed his eyes he could see her again, feel her under his hands, her amazing responsiveness, fire and passion.

He moaned and scrubbed off, before too many thoughts of
her drove him mad, or to needing another hand job. Drying off
quickly, Jack glanced at his phone, saw a couple of texts from a
female friend looking for company, and smiled.

*Yes, that's it. A nice night with a different one – that will
drive her out of my head. Someone easy, simple, who doesn't
require more than just a quick fuck.*

He dressed in jeans and a t-shirt sporting the logo of a
friend's brewery, kept going downstairs, straight for the liquor
cabinet. The night had cooled, and he was determined to enjoy the
damn patio furniture his decorator had chosen, raping his bank
account in the process. He poured himself a double bourbon,
opened the French doors, stepped onto the paver stones and dropped
into a cushy chair.

Images of Sara rose unbidden - across from him, in his
house, her eyes bright with laughter, wine glass in hand, soft tanned
legs tucked up under her as they talked. He downed the bourbon in
one fiery gulp. His phone buzzed across the table but he ignored it.
She'd never call. Not tonight. She got what she wanted and could
ignore him until the next time.

*You have to say something to her, dumbass. Women need
to be communicated with, remember?*

*Yeah, the last time I was the Great Communicator with a
woman she ... oh fuck it.*

After his healthy pour of Kentucky's best, he relaxed. Then
suddenly his throat closed up in panic, his heart pounded faster,
denying what his bourbon-infused brain was telling him – that he
might very well be in love with Sara Thornton. In one quick motion,
Jack stood, scooped up keys and phone and headed for his front
door on a mission to talk to someone who might set him straight.

As he pulled into a parking spot at the Big House Brewing
Company's tap room, Jack smiled at the sight of his buddy's vintage
Jaguar crouched near the door. He smiled to himself. Evan Adams
had car lust nearly as bad as Jack did, one of the many things that
had kept them close beyond law school.

He slammed his corvette door shut and glanced around the
lot, noting a few other cars he recognized. Evan had opened Ann

Arbor's only Tap Room about six years ago, giving everything he had to his dream of brewing craft beer and serving it in his own space to friends, beer snobs, and geeks alike. Their company had fast become a regional success story. However, at that moment, Jack needed his friend's ear.

He pulled the door open, and the unfamiliar but pleasant odors of brewery operations flowed around him and out into the humid night. Suzanne, Evan's business partner and another of Jack's old friends from college, spotted him and waved from behind the bar. He smiled at her red-headed perkiness and took a seat, leaving two chairs empty between him and the nearest customer.

Checking his phone again, he noted a couple of texts from some chick he could probably call later if he wanted – but nothing from Sara. As he looked up, he saw several people in the room he'd sold houses to and reflected that he really ought to get out there and talk to them but was somehow frozen in place. He put his phone in his pocket and leaned on the bar hoping to stay anonymous a bit longer.

"Gordon!" he turned at the sound of Evan's voice. "What the hell? It's nine o'clock Friday night and you're alone?" Evan walked around behind the long length of bar and stood in front of Jack. "You're destroying my image of you man, I have to tell ya." He smiled and poured him their hoppiest beer – Jack's favorite.

He accepted the beer and drained half of it. Evan raised an eyebrow then busied himself wiping off the glassware drying by the sink. The additional alcohol started to work its magic. He took a deep breath and leaned back in his chair, watching the Tigers pull to a five-to-five tie with the Indians in silence. Suzanne appeared at his elbow and he hugged her small frame, his mind drifting to their short time as a couple.

Jesus Gordon, you are really an expert at letting the good ones get away.

He shook his head. Suzanne pulled back from his embrace and stared at him, suspicion in her eyes.

"Okay Jack, who is she?"

He glared at her. "What? Don't you work here? I'm telling your boss you're fraternizing with customers." He turned back around and leaned on his elbows so she would stop staring at him.

Evan got a fresh glass, filled it to the brim and put it in front of him. Suzanne had a knack for figuring out what was wrong with someone, sometimes even before they did. Jack slammed the second beer back and she caught his eye. Evan put a glass of ice water down on the bar.

"Chaser," he muttered.

"Thanks." He looked up at the industrial ceiling. "So, I have two different women wanting me to meet them out tonight," he began. Suzanne snorted in disgust.

"And your point is what," Evan made a swipe at the bar.

"What the hell is wrong with me?" Jack asked the ceiling. "I mean she's a colleague for Christ's sake, nearly ten years younger than me." He watched his friends exchange a look.

Jack ran a hand down his face. "One more," he pushed the empty glass towards Evan. "But only if you join me."

Evan poured three beers. Jack raised his. "Here's to being nearly forty, gainfully employed, and alone."

"And rich as God, don't forget that. Oh, and with a black book any man would murder for." Evan clinked his glass against Jack's.

"And a jerk, don't forget that." Suzanne joined them and smiled as Jack rolled his eyes. "You know, you're supposed to savor this beer, boys. It's not PBR." She took Jack's face between her hands and forced him to look at her. He squinted and acknowledged he probably should slow down a little after a double bourbon and three strong beers on an empty stomach.

"I don't know what your problem is Gordon or who this colleague is that's got you tied up in knots but don't sell yourself short because you're 'alone'." She gave him a soft kiss on the lips. "Sometimes 'alone' isn't a bad way to be. Something you ought to get better at maybe. Keep yourself out of trouble that way." She stood and took her pint glass with her. "I gotta work. You boys carry on without me but try to behave."

Jack watched her walk around to the far end of the bar. "We both missed the boat with that one." He turned to Evan. "What the fuck was your problem? I mean, I understand my own commitment phobia but you. . ." Jack trailed off and finished off his third brew.

"Oh, wait, I know, you've got that uber smoking hot beer sales chick now, don't you?" Jack pointed at Evan. "You slam dunked on that one."

"Yeah, Julie is great," Evan admitted. "But what the hell is with you man?"

"Oh, fuck, I don't know," Jack stared at the baseball game on the TV behind his friend. "This girl, she's up in my head in a way I. . ." He ran a hand down his face. "She's perfect for me. Driven, focused, not clingy, a goddamned tiger between the sheets, and independent as hell. The whole package."

"Uh, yeah, and you're here getting drunk with me on a summer night why exactly?"

Evan refilled his water glass. "Wait, is this the one you were jacking off over on our Up North trip? Holy shit, that one?" He laughed as Jack nodded. "Jesus dude, I haven't seen you this worked up since, well, ever. You aren't thinking of doing anything stupid are you?" Evan frowned at him.

"Hey, you haven't...." he looked around. "She's not...oh fuck. She is, isn't she?" Evan sucked back half his beer and stared at Jack. "Look, Jack. I don't know if you realize this but you've got that look. You know, the one you get when..." He looked over Jack's shoulder again. "You do know that Julie and I..." Jack stared into his friend's eyes. "We, ah, joined the club again. Downtown. I mean, if you want to come back."

"No, no, it's not like that." He closed his eyes. *Never again.* "She's pretty amazing but not...I mean, I can't."

Evan raised an eyebrow. The two men had spent several years in high demand as Masters at an exclusive downtown club. Jack knew the guy had read him. It was built into their DNA. He put his head on his arms. "I won't." he muttered.

Evan slapped his shoulder. "That's cool. But you should know that I am having a kick ass time getting back into it." He kept his voice low. "And I can read you like a fucking book Gordon. It's back. You should go with it."

Jack glanced at his phone for hundredth time, noted somewhat blearily that he had another text from some woman he couldn't even remember. Apparently he'd gone down on her in such a memorable way that she wanted more, tonight, if possible. He threw the phone onto the bar's surface and made his way to the men's room. When he returned, he'd somehow become attached to a tall, exotic looking woman. Evan raised an eyebrow and Jack shrugged.

"Let me buy, um, what did you say your name was honey," Jack leaned into her neck and she giggled. Her body was the opposite of Sara's – tall, angular, sharp.

"Okay Jack, let's have one more and call it a night."

Jack pulled a chair near his and stared hard at the woman who took a seat in it."Hey, you know, you are hot, but.," Jack leaned away and grabbed his phone. "Damn. What the fuck is her problem anyway," he threw the device back down on the concrete surface. Evan pulled the beer away from him.

"Hey buddy, have you eaten much today?" He put the water glass in its place.

"So, Jack, what's her name?" Suzanne ignored the very drunk, very tall woman leaning on Jack's shoulder.

"Sara," he said into the woman's hair. She lifted her head and crashed right into Jack's face. "Jesus!" He clutched at his nose.

"Hey, my name's Heather, asshole," she smiled at him.

"Sara Thornton," he said to Suzanne, ignoring the woman glaring at him.

Suzanne frowned.

"Yeah, sorry sweets. Blake's sister." He had his arm back around Heather and his lips on her neck. Evan cleared his throat. Suzanne's face reddened. "Small world, eh?" She opened her mouth to speak. "Whoa baby, whoa," Jack removed Heather's hand as it settled on his zipper. She giggled and tried to kiss him but he turned away. Suzanne stomped off.

Evan came around from behind the bar and pulled Jack out of her clutches. "Okay, let's call it a night, eh kids?" He helped Jack to his feet. "I've called a cab for you Gordon, and one for you too dear." He flashed a smile at the woman still sitting dejectedly at the bar.

"Thanks, sorry, I…um, thanks." Jack was no lightweight. But something had happened to him tonight he could not explain. He was drunk, but misery settled around his heart until he had a thought.

"It's not like you haven't done the same for me you know." Evan guided Jack out to the waiting taxi making sure Heather did not climb in next to him. He gave the cab driver Jack's address and slammed the door shut but leaned into the open window and grabbed Jack's shoulder. "Go home, sleep it off, we'll talk more tomorrow."

The distinct odor of taxi pierced Jack's beer foggy brain. He gave the cabbie an address that was not his and fell back against the seat, unsure yet utterly content at the same time.

Sara sipped her wine as her favorite playlist blasted through the condo. She tapped around on the laptop, killing time on blogs and Facebook, bragging about her latest real estate triumphs, bullshitting about how great she felt right now. She glanced at the nearly empty bottle on the coffee table.

Wow, way to be a loser and drink nearly an entire bottle by yourself.

Setting the computer aside, she took the almost empty bottle into the kitchen. Ignoring the usual chaos that reigned in that room, she found a spot for the bottle and glass. As she reached for a water bottle a loud prolonged banging on her door caused her to knock her not-quite-empty glass to the floor, shattering it and sending dark purple liquid flying across the room.

"Shit," She stared at the mess in disbelief as the knocking continued.

Who the hell?

"Coming already, keep your pants on. Ow! Christ!" She yelped at sudden pain in her foot, hopped over to the door and glared out of the peephole. Jack leaned on the pillar outside her condo, a wide grin on his face. Her scalp prickled as she leaned her head against the door.

Don't let him in... Don't let him in... Don't let him in...

She unlatched the door, and opened it a crack.

"What do you want?"

He put a hand on the doorjamb. She could smell the beer on him. "Oh, I was just in the neighborhood, and thought I'd stop in."

Sara peered behind him. "What did you do, walk?" she demanded.

"Nope, taxi," he put his other hand out to cup her chin. Sara shivered at his touch. "May I come in?"

"Only if you help clean up the mess you caused." She swung the door open. He was drunk, but her foot hurt and was bleeding and she didn't feel like standing here arguing with him. Turning back to the small dining area, she hobbled over to the table, sat and inspected the glass sticking out from her arch. The place was a wreck, as usual, but fuck him if he cared. She didn't. As she prepared to yank out the shard Jack's large hand covered hers.

"Wait, babe, where's your first aid stuff," he insisted, striding into the kitchen as if he owned it. "You don't want to do that until you have a Band-Aid handy." He started to open drawers and doors. She frowned as he grabbed a paper towel and ran it under the faucet before returning to sit in front of her, bandage, paper towel and ancient tube of first aid cream in hand. "Here, let me," he brushed her hand away. Sara stared at him, then sat back and let him put her foot on his lap, ignoring the zinging sensations his touch always caused. He removed the shard, pressed the wet towel over the cut. She bit her lip against the pain. A contented feeling settled over her like a blanket at the concept of him, helping her, taking care of her. She'd always pictured herself in an equal partnership with a man someday, had never fantasized about being coddled or "taken care of." She had to remind herself to breathe over the extreme compulsions to climb up into his lap.

They sat in silence as his large masculine presence overpowered her small, chaotic space. After a minute, he removed the bloody towel, spread some of ointment on the bandage and placed it over her arch, then ran a hand across the top of her foot and up her calf. She bent her leg and let him, relishing his nearness, before she snapped to and yanked her foot off his lap. Her every nerve ending commanded her to wrap herself around him, feel him, kiss him; anything to keep him here.

No, Sara, get a fucking grip! Go clean up the mess and get him out of here.

She turned towards the kitchen without a word, determined to get the spill and glass cleaned up and ignore him until he told her why he was here in the middle of the night.

"Um, Sara," he muttered.

"What?" It came out harsher than she wanted.

"You might want to put on some shoes or something." He indicated the glass shards twinkling on the white linoleum floor. Sara squeezed her eyes shut to keep from speaking. "You're welcome, by the way," Jack said as he followed her into the least-used room in her home.

"Thanks," she muttered as she found a pair of flip-flops, her broom and dustpan, and started sweeping up the worst of the glass. Jack walked past her, opened up the cabinet beneath her sink, and emerged with some cleaning spray. "You don't have to do that." She watched him remove the burgundy-colored Rorschach test covering the wall.

"No, it's okay, my fault, like you said," he grinned at her and her heart skipped a beat. She bent back to her task. He gave the surface one last swipe and put the cleaner back where he found it and looked around in the obvious places for a garbage bin.

"Oh, yeah. Here," she plucked the wine stained towel out of his hand crossed the kitchen in three strides. Opening the door between it and the small garage, she deposited everything into the bin she had put outside earlier that morning, rather than to try to sort out why it had stunk so badly. Her head spun from a combination of too much wine, too little food and Jack's presence. Shoulders squared, she re-entered the kitchen only to find it empty.

"Jack," she peered into the living room and saw him, feet propped on the coffee table, her computer on his lap. Anger surged up from her throat. "Find anything you like?" She plopped on the couch next to him and retrieved the laptop wincing at the images from The Suite's website that she'd been studying again, alongside the Wiki entry she originally found when she Googled "BDSM."

He put his hands behind his head and looked up at her ceiling, unnerving her with silence. She curled her feet under her and retreated to the opposite end of the leather surface. "Well," she tried to control the tremor in her voice. "Why are you here? Lose everything at poker night and need a loan? I'm busy, if you must know. I've got the potential for three great transactions from one referral, but they are fucking commission cutters and I'm trying to figure it out," She stopped as Jack reached out a hand and put his finger over her lips.

"Sara, this is not something you study on Wikipedia. It's something you either get or you don't. Something you want or…" He flopped back and looked up at her ceiling. Mortified, she started to stand up, ready to order him out. His hand on her bare leg stopped her. "I don't mean you shouldn't launch headlong into a lifestyle without understanding. I just, here, give me that back a minute," he gestured for her computer, typed in an address and handed it back to her. A site called "leather and roses" appeared, free of any weird porn-like photos that she kept finding in her search for serious information about the psychology of a submissive. She bit her lip then looked up at him.

He rubbed his forehead with both hands before standing up to head back into the kitchen. "I need water." She stared at the screen, realizing this was exactly what she'd been seeking for the last week with no luck. An email dinged, making her change focus. The damn sellers again, telling her they'd only pay her five percent since she was "getting" two houses to list out of their deal.

Sara resolved then and there to not let him lay a finger on her again no matter how badly her body clamored for it. She was selling herself short with this guy out of pure animal lust. It was time to get some control back. She had no time for all this crazy fetish lifestyle crap.

She turned the music back on, as she made the calculations to justify her company's marketing fee to the cheapskates who wanted her to work for essentially nothing to sell their houses. When her fingers shook and her skin prickled, she realized something. Jack had returned to the room.

She ignored him, with some effort, until he squatted down in front of her and took the computer off her lap. Hands clasped together, she let her struggle to stay angry take over – it was the only thing keeping her from launching herself into his arms. She could smell the combination of beer, his citrusy cologne, and lust wrap around her. Her foot throbbed where she'd skewered it. She tried to calm her racing heartbeat, but would not meet his eyes. He sighed, stood back up, sat next to her and proceeded to give her a lecture on why her services were worth a full six percent of the sale price. Sara listened, awed by his logical argument.

"Wait, Jack, let me get this down," she reached for her computer, intent on capturing the words tumbling out of his mouth. After typing furiously, asking questions, and formulating her argument for nearly thirty minutes, she closed the computer with a snap and looked up at him. His eyes shone as he studied her. Nervous and uncomfortable all of a sudden under his gaze, she tugged at her ponytail and started to ease away from him. Without a word, he reached for her arm and pulled her closer.

You want this Sara, New Sara cooed in her ear. *Let him do what he came here to do.*

Jack kept tugging at her arm in silence, until she was nestled in his lap, his arms circling her body, his lips near her ear. He released her hair from its holder and ran his hands through it, brushing it back from her face.

She took a breath as his mouth hovered over hers and resisted the urge to grasp his neck and make him kiss her. He brushed his lips over hers before retreating to stare at the ceiling again. Sara let herself remain curled in his lap, breathing him in. Let her mind touch briefly on the protected sensation she had in his arms before scurrying away in terror.

Jack is not your protector. He only wants to get laid. And you keep letting him. Her brain kept up the lecturing and she stiffened in his arms as he spoke.

"Sara, I'm sorry," he said to the ceiling.

"Huh?"

"Let me finish." He leveled his deep blue gaze at her and she fell into it, unwilling to move from her spot cradled in his arms. Her skin broke out in goose bumps at his next words.

"You deserve better than how I've been treating you," he held her gaze. "You're special. I'm a shit. Not a nice guy. I should leave you alone." He shook his head as if trying to clear it. "But I can't leave you alone. I just can't," he paused. "And I've had way too much to drink." His jaw clenched as he trailed off.

She extracted herself from his arms, with reluctance, but needing to get her bearings outside of the circle of his scent. He was admitting stuff she had longed to hear, but somehow it was freaking her out instead of soothing her. She sat beside him and leaned forward. He joined her, mirroring her posture at the edge of the couch.

"I'm not an easy guy to love, or even really like," he said to his clasped hands. Sara's scalp prickled. "I know that, and I won't give you a shit load of sad sack stories about how my parents ignored or criticized me into the man I am now." He snorted. "Hell, I'd barely tolerate me if I didn't have to." Sara felt his gaze on her but kept her eyes trained on the floor. "What I know right now is that there is something about you, Sara Thornton, that has me spinning in circles. It pisses me the fuck off, if you must know," he leaned back again and pulled her next to him. She started to talk but he silenced her by pulling her face to his for a brief kiss. "Shut up, let me finish," he muttered, taking his lips from hers.

Sara started to stand up but Jack pulled her back. "Sit down, please, I. . ." he stopped. "I can't even do this right."

Sara bit back the urge to speak.

"I have thousands of people who consider me a 'friend' – am invited to events, parties and shit every single weekend – but I only have two maybe three people on the planet I ever really talk to." He swallowed and turned his face to hers as they sat side by side on the couch. "I need something more. And I don't understand why you keep pulling away from me." He stood up towering over her. "And this thing that I do. I'm not convinced it's good or even right, but you bring out urges in me I haven't felt for years." He turned and headed into the kitchen presumably for more water.

When he didn't return for a few minutes, Sara walked to the doorway and watched as he sat at her small breakfast bar running his hands through his hair. Her heart raced again as she walked over to him and put a hand on his shoulder. He grabbed it, kissed her palm and stood up in one smooth motion tugging her to him. She sighed as he covered her mouth with his but broke the contact and pushed back on his chest to hold him at arm's length.

"Jack," she said, fighting New Sara's urge to straddle him and make him carry her to bed. "I, um, I'm not a coddler, you know? I've been on my own long enough that I buy myself flowers, make my own pancake breakfasts, and am more than a little emotionally constipated. I don't know how to give up control if you must know. And the fact that I even want to…" He moved her hands from their position on his shoulders up around his neck and she melted into him again. "You scare me," she muttered into his chest. "I'm actually terrified of how I feel about you. I don't want to get hurt." Tears stung her eyes but she clenched them back. "I don't know what I want. But I know you've done something to me. And it pisses me the fuck off too." She sighed, loving he smell of him so close. "And as for the other, well, it scares me too. But it fascinates me at the same time. Kind of like you."

"Well, hell darlin' that makes two of us," he whispered into her hair. "I guess we'll just have to work through our fear together, eh? I'm willing to try, if you are." He kissed her before she could answer. She yelped when he scooped her up. "Where the hell is the bedroom?" Her brain spun, as she relished his lips on hers and his words in her ears.

Could it be, really? Jack Gordon wants me? For what? A girlfriend? A sub? Holy shit Blake is going to kill me.

Jack put her down and sat on the bed, tugging her onto his lap, so close she no choice but to straddle him. He smiled when she pushed him back before crawling up to his lips, grasping her ass against the stiffening under his zipper.

"Jesus, woman, I have no business getting hard, I am so goddamned drunk, but you," he growled into her ear. "You could make a dead man come, to quote Jagger and company," he yanked her t-shirt up and pulled a nipple into his mouth.

"Jack," Sara started, eyes closed as her pussy clenched in anticipation. "Are you gonna remember any of this tomorrow?" She sat up and glared into his darkening eyes. He propped himself on his elbows.

"Yes," he said, simply and pulled her back down, rolled her over and held her wrists down on the bed. She squirmed in anticipation. He took a minute to kiss her deeply, his tongue invading her mouth, before moving his lips down her neck, between her breasts, and pulling her nipples erect with his lips and teeth. He shoved a thigh between her legs and something primal in her made her rub her now aching clit against him.

"Ah, Jack, Jesus," she called out and yanked her arms out from his grasp and buried her hands in his course hair. He kept sucking each nipple, sending blasts of erotic sensation straight to her core. "I need you inside me," she demanded into his hair. "Now. I've waited long enough."

He grinned against her breast, pulled her shorts and panties aside in one quick movement and plunged two fingers inside her velvet depths. "No need to wait baby. Let me have it." His words and touch set off a hair trigger orgasm and she yelled in pleasure as her pussy clutched at his fingers and gushed moisture onto his hand. Alarmed to find herself near tears, she sighed. Jack removed his fingers from her body and put them in his mouth.

"Okay I think you're really ready for me now," he started to unzip his shorts but stopped. "Oh, shit, I, um, I didn't bring anything." She grinned at him.

"Never fear lover," she sat up, unzipped his shorts and yanked them and his boxer briefs down over his hips, releasing his shaft. "I'm gonna return the favor," he laid back as she drew his thickness into her mouth, pulling, sucking, relishing the taste and essence of him.

"Ah, sweet Jesus," he fisted his hands in her hair as she cupped his balls in her hand, using her other hand to run up and down his shaft under her lips. She dipped her tongue into the slit, sucking down the pre-come that moistened him, licking around the edges of his head, bringing him nearly to the brink. His hips started bucking into her. But he stopped, and pulled her back up, forcing her to stop. "No, I want to come inside you, now," he declared. "But I…"

"I'll rustle up some protection, you get all the way undressed." Sara pulled her clothes off under his admiring gaze and checked her bedside drawer. Nothing. She ran into the living room to look in her purse. Empty. At the last minute, she ran into the bathroom, scrabbled around in the drawers and came up with a condom packet. She stopped to run a brush through her hair and grinned at herself in the mirror.

Jack Gordon eh? Well, at least she'd always have great real estate advice when she needed it, not to mention some of the best fucking she'd ever…

The sound of a massive snore rolled through the room, stopping her in her tracks. She sighed and opened the door, leaning in the entry as the man who had sort of confessed that he might very possibly love her lay on his back, completely naked, his mouth open, sound asleep.

Sara jerked awake to what sounded like cars crashing and loud cursing from the vicinity of her kitchen. She sat up, rubbed her eyes and took in the rumpled side of the bed where Jack had passed out on top of the covers. Glancing down at her naked body, she smiled with the memory of last night's actual discussion. He must be trying to find the coffee pot or something in there. A nearly fruitless endeavor she knew. She laid back on her pillow and let her mind drift back to the confessions they'd made to each other. The cursing got louder and moved towards the bedroom.

"Sara!" Jack barked. "I'm late! I'm supposed to be touring a Ford exec in forty-five minutes." He stood there completely naked still, magnificent cock at half-mast. He ran a hand over his face once, found his underwear and pulled them on. "Do you have any decent coffee? Never mind, I'll get some later," he started to stalk out of the room. She sat up, alarmed.

He had forgotten. She knew it. She tried to quell crushing disappointment. He stopped in the doorway, put both hands on either side of the jamb, and took a deep breath. "I, um, need a ride home. Do you mind?" he asked without looking at her.

Sara rolled out of bed, pulled on jeans, a t-shirt, and her flip-flops, wincing as her sore foot made contact with the floor. She glared at Jack as he fiddled with email on his Blackberry, forcing back tears.

God damn fucking asshole, he's done it to me again. Sara, you are a fool.

The face in the mirror mocked her as she brushed her teeth and pulled her hair back. Jack blocked her way out of the bedroom and for a brief moment; she thought he was going to reach out for her, but he merely stepped aside and followed her out into the living room. She grabbed purse and keys and stomped out the front door, not watching to see if he followed. They screeched out of her parking lot, silence gathering force between them.

Jack gave her his address and said nothing else. Sara gripped the steering wheel with white knuckles, willing him to speak. She'd be damned if she would first. She pulled up in front of his bungalow in the affluent neighborhood near the central campus, and kept her eyes straight ahead. Jack sat, unmoving, one hand on the door handle. He put the other on her shoulder.

"Sara," he said, quietly. "I, you, I mean, we. . . shit," he muttered. "I'm late, I really have got to go. But I remember what I said last night, okay?" He put a finger under her chin and turned her face to his before giving her a kiss of such tenderness and feeling that she nearly wept with relief. "We have to talk more, and we will," he said as he brushed her nose and forehead with his lips. "I'll call you this afternoon." He ran a weary hand over his eyes and through his thick hair, making it stand up in spikes. "I've got a stupid golf outing tomorrow, but if this day doesn't go too long let's have dinner." He jumped out of the car and ran towards his house, disappearing into the side door as her nerve endings hummed with unmet need. The anticipation of conversations with her brother that had "Jack" and "boyfriend" in the same sentence made her a little dizzy. She sighed, put the car in gear and headed home.

CHAPTER TEN

"This is Sara Thornton, how can I help you," she chirped into the phone the next morning as she took a floor call. It had been a late night and not an entirely satisfying one. Jack had called at nine o'clock after keeping her posted via text during his tour. He sounded exhausted after an entire day spent nursing a raging hangover while shuttling a top-level executive around with his high-maintenance spouse and two annoying children. He'd been apologetic and contrite but begged off anything more than falling straight into bed.

"I owe you one baby," he'd muttered into her ear. "And you know I will make good on it." Sara had bit the inside of her cheek so hard to keep from filling the silence she tasted blood. "I'll pick you up at seven tomorrow night. Dress up." he insisted before signing off.

She'd set her phone down on the coffee table, called for her favorite pizza, and ordered a movie on demand. She had woken up in a sweating, hyperventilating heap on the floor beside the couch, the movie playing in an endless loop. She couldn't recall the nightmare that had caused her such panic but took a hot shower to calm down and then fell face first into bed, not moving until the alarm went off at six a.m. for her morning run.

She felt re-energized afterwards, showered, and headed into the office. No word from Jack yet, but that wasn't unusual. He'd said he had a golf outing, wouldn't be able to talk all day, so she mentally inventoried her closet for something great to wear on their date tonight.

Their Date...Sara flushed with anticipation and relief. He'd finally done it. Feeling liberated, strong and utterly terrified in equal measure, she waded through emails, chatted with the secretary about various bits of company gossip, listening carefully for any tidbits about Jack the girl might share. By the time she got the first floor call the clock read noon, the end of her shift. The buyer on the other end of the phone wanted to see a listing today, in an hour, out in the township.

Sara sighed, picturing her afternoon spent on a most likely useless trek out to meet a less-than-qualified buyer. She set the meeting, printed out a few more listings in the price range and general vicinity to take with her. Then finished off the work on transactions she had in the pipeline, smiling when she realized next month would be her most lucrative one yet. Her phone buzzed with a text and she smiled anticipating Jack's missive. She frowned at the unfamiliar number.

"Hey. It's Craig. Can you cover me for about thirty minutes? I'm supposed to be there at noon, but am gonna be late."

"Sure, but I got a last minute showing at one so don't be much later." She hit "save contact" and entered his name, the image of his tanned face and long blond hair wavering in her vision. He had proven to be a very quick study, and had picked up the real estate lingo and processes with little apparent effort. Their one close encounter had made for some awkwardness, but he'd effectively ignored her since then, so she let it drop.

His lazy smile and easy-going manner, not to mention absolutely adorable southern accent and smoking hot body had quickly made him a favorite among the women. Sara thought she'd heard he had already gone out with an admin at their corporate office.

At the rumble of his motorcycle outside, Sara grabbed her phone and keys and headed for the back door. The vision that greeted her as she exited made her stumble over the sidewalk. Craig had dismounted his bike and was taking his helmet off, shaking his dark-blond hair out and pulling off his Ray-Bans. Sara took in the rumpled khakis hugging his ass and the sinfully tight black t-shirt emphasizing the smooth strength of his arms. He wasn't bulked up but was deliciously toned. He grabbed a button down shirt out of the compartment behind his seat and was shoving his arms in it when he turned and stopped as he saw Sara standing there staring at him. He grinned and she nearly melted.

Good Lord, he is like a fucking Greek God or something. She stopped herself and smiled back at him, her heart beating faster.

"About time, cutie," she called out, covering her discomfort.

"Sorry, late night, had a gig over in Grosse Pointe," he said, indicating one of the farthest Northeast Detroit suburbs.

Jesus, he probably has amazing hands.

Sara shook her head to rid herself of the image of them on his guitar. "No problem. Had a last minute floor call is all. Some guy wanting to see some stupid house way out on Willis Road"

Craig narrowed his eyes at her. "You're going? Alone? Is that safe?"

"Oh it'll be fine. But thanks for asking," she waved her hand as she turned to her car. "Hope you get more calls than I did!" Within a minute, she got another text from him.

"If there is a problem text me 911 and the address."

Sara smiled and made her way out to the house. The supposed buyer stood her up for nearly twenty minutes which annoyed her but she pasted on her best smile as she held the door open for him. Within about ten seconds, every inner alarm she had started clanging. He was dressed well enough, tall, with a baseball cap, jeans and a t-shirt. But his eyes traveled over her frame in a thoroughly disconcerting and inappropriate way.

Get a grip Sara. It's nothing, show the house and be done.

But her nerves kept buzzing and she automatically took the precautions that had been drummed into them – made him lead the way into each room, standing in the hall, feigning a couple of phone calls, remaining in the kitchen while he traversed the large overgrown yard. She immediately tried to call Jack as soon as he walked out the door. His voicemail picked up so she sent him a text: "911 1750 Willis Rd." and then sent the same message to Craig.

The guy wandered back into the house after about ten minutes. He took a step too close to her and she eased away. She blew out a breath as he continued past her down to the basement. She started towards the front door after he'd spent nearly ten more minutes down there.

"Hey, um Sara, could you come here and show me what this leak is," the creep called from the basement.

Yeah, as if. I'm out of here.

Sara focused on getting to the front door and down the porch steps towards her car when she felt a rough hand grip her arm. She pulled out of his grasp and he grinned at her.

"You aren't being a very good realtor now are you," he grabbed for her again. An adrenaline rush kicked in as she rushed down the steps when he caught the tail of her silk shirt. The ripping sound sent a bolt of terror through her brain. Her yell cut through the country road's quiet when he turned and shoved her up against her car, so hard her head ricocheted against the metal, bringing instant stars to her vision.

Channeling Blake's self-defense class she slammed her knee up between his legs but he sidestepped her and put a hand over her mouth. He yelped when she bit down on the palm covering her mouth, wrenched her arm behind her back and turned her to face the car.

"Bad realtor," he muttered into her ear. He yanked her arm up so far she screamed in pain. "Shut up goddamn it." The guy had his lips so near her ear she could smell the rank odor of cigarettes and unwashed skin. His hand mashed against her ear. The car's hot metal seared her cheek. She could smell her own sour, sweaty fear. The unmistakable sensation of an erection pressed into her body. The guy's breath permeated her nostrils. Her brain was on overdrive but he had her completely immobile, pinned against her car door.

She opened her mouth to talk, beg. She felt a rough hand on her leg, shoving her skirt up. Her flight instinct kicked in. She would not stand here and be abused by this asshole. He yanked her away from the car, the air a relief to her scorched skin, quickly replaced by a sting of pain when he backhanded her so forcefully her neck jerked back, one hand still gripping her arm so hard it almost hurt worse than the blow.

"Bitch. Now be still." He whipped her back around, shoved her against the car door again and put a large hand around her neck. "Yell again, and I'll squeeze." Sara's fuddled brain registered him fumbling around with his zipper.

Tears leaked from her eyes as her mind slowly processed that her own desire for a sale might cost her life. She sobbed and tried to relax so whatever he did wouldn't hurt as much.

The roar of a motorcycle engine tore through the quiet, gravel flew from under Craig's wheels as he spun up to where the attacker had Sara pinned. He squeezed her throat so hard the world started to go black from the outside in. Then he grunted and was suddenly gone.

Sara landed on her hands and knees sucking in deep drafts of air, heard, rather than saw, flesh hitting flesh. Once she managed to unfreeze her limbs and turn around, she took in the sight of the guy on the ground face down, blood darkening the area around his head. Craig was crouched on his back, had his arms pinned. When he looked at her, the edges of her vision went black. She could hear the sounds of a police siren somewhere from a long way away as she crumpled to the gravel.

The first thing she saw was his deep brown eyes full of concern. Strong hands lifted her up and she let herself be pulled into Craig's embrace. Strange scents assaulted her; a combination of sweat, starch and something like bleach surrounded her as she clutched at his shirt, sobbing with residual terror. He held her close and ran a hand over her hair.

"It's okay Sara, I'm here. He's gone. It's gonna be fine." His soft, melodious voice soothed her. She took a shuddering breath and let go of him to rub at her eyes but nearly fell down again as her knees shook too violently to hold her up. Craig led her to the porch steps. Her head throbbed with pain and she trembled uncontrollably as the adrenaline whooshed out of her body. He sat and put an arm around her shoulders.

"Relax, it's over," he muttered into her ear. She nodded but burst into tears, and leaned into him noting the bleach smell again coming from his soft blond hair. Craig stood up and blocked her view when the cops marched the would-be rapist to the patrol car. While she laid her head on her knees and tried not to throw up, they shoved him into the back, conferred with another set of uniforms that had arrived in the meantime and made way for the paramedics. Sara waved the medic away. "I'm fine, just scared," she declared, not wanting anyone in her space but Craig.

He sat beside her again and tipped her face up to look at him. His dark eyes blazed with intensity.

"Sara, you took a hit, remember, let them check it out," he insisted running a finger over her stinging cheek. She clutched at his sleeve.

"Okay, but stay here with me." He nodded at the paramedic and kept an arm around her while they did their concussion check. They declared her fine, if severely shaken up. After rubbing some ointment on her sore cheek, they gave her orders to get to the ER if she got really nauseous. As the man walked towards the ambulance, Jack's corvette wheeled into the driveway with a roar. Sara gasped with alarm and Craig kept a tight arm around her. Jack leapt out of the car and ran over to them clad in full golf outing gear, complete with spiked shoes.

"What the hell happened," he glared around at the police cars and ambulance. Sara stood on shaky legs and he crushed her to him. "I'm sorry. I didn't get your message. I was out on the course," he ran a hand down her hair and her back. Sara's body convulsed with tremors again. He pushed her away, touched the crumpled skirt, pulled her shirt together. "Dear God, did he hurt you?" He gripped her arms, eyes wild with fury. He looked around at the cop car. "Hey, where is this asshole," he yelled to them. "Sit, here, I'll be right back." Craig hadn't moved so she sat back next to him, soothed by the warmth of his body.

Jack stomped over to the group of cops conferring next to their car. He waved his arms around and yelled until one of them put an arm around his shoulders and led him away. Sara hiccuped again and laid her head on Craig's shoulder. The cop and Jack appeared in front of them.

"Sara," Jack said drawing her to her feet. "You need to answer some questions then I'll take you home," he glanced at Craig and stuck out his hand. "The police tell me you were the one who alerted them. You probably saved her life. Thanks, a lot." He pumped Craig's hand and slapped him on the shoulder. "Seriously, thank you," he looked at Sara and pulled her close. Craig nodded at Jack and looked hard at Sara.

"I told you not to come out here you know," he reminded her, his gaze still full of worry.

She pulled herself free of Jack's arm and flung herself around Craig's neck, noting that laundry fresh smell that permeated him and the feel of his strong shoulders under her grasp.

"Thank you," she sobbed as tears started flowing again. "I promise to listen next time."

"No, you probably won't but that's what makes you, you." Craig grinned at her. Jack's eyes narrowed at the young blonde man as he mounted his Ducati, set his helmet in place, and waved before pulling out onto the country road. He tugged her back down on the step and sat with her as she gave her report to the cop. She broke down, describing how the man had chased her out of the house and slammed her against her own car. Jack blew out a puff of air and held her closer. She could sense his anger as if it were a wild animal circling their ankles, ready to pounce.

Once the questioning was finished, Jack tucked her into the passenger seat of his car and shut the door before conferring with the cops one last time. He gestured towards the man in the back of the official vehicle. Sara stared straight ahead, numb and shivering as Jack got in, turned the key and pulled out of the driveway, pointing the car towards Ann Arbor. She watched as his jaw flexed and clenched.

"What made you think coming out here alone after a single phone call was the smart thing to do," he asked as he shifted gears. She stared at him. Her face flushed. "That goes against everything you're trained to do, Sara, goddamn it!"

"You know what, I was just attacked. Nearly raped. Save the lecture for another time." She reached for the phone Craig had pressed back into her hand after he retrieved it from the gravel. She hit Blake's quick dial number.

Jack sighed and glanced at her as she told her brother what had happened. After filing her ear he demanded to talk to Jack, so she handed the phone over. Jack had a brief conversation with him, gave Blake his address, and handed it back to her, his face grim. "That went well." He sighed.

"Yeah, he's a little overprotective. This is exactly the sort of thing that makes him nuts." She closed her eyes and realized she could just as easily be referring to her relationship with Jack as to her recent brush with sexual assault, as a reason for Blake to go ballistic.

Tears formed, and she let them flow down her still smarting face. Jack put a hand on her leg. "Jesus Christ Sara, please don't do that to me again," his voice was rough. Sara took a long, shuddering breath and put her hand on his. He twined his fingers in hers, bringing her hand to his lips. "When I saw the ambulance I...." he shook his head. "Look, just use common sense, please." He let her hand go to downshift as they approached Ann Arbor.

Both Rob and Blake were waiting at Jack's house when they pulled in. Sara fell into their arms. "Want me to take you home?" Blake whispered in her ear.

"I want a stiff drink, then I want to lie down, I don't care where," she declared as tears threatened again. Her knees started to tremble again.

"C'mon in all of you," Jack gestured towards his house. Blake shook his head, but Rob put a hand on his arm. "Rob," Jack stuck out his hand. "Long time no see."

Rob smiled and shook his hand. "Yeah, it has been." Sara looked at each of them arranged around Jack's large front porch like it was the fucking OK Corral.

"Stand down for Christ's sake, and take me inside. I need a shower, and never want to see these clothes again." she stomped towards the front door as the men stood and watched her before following her inside.

Sara let the water pour over her head, trying to shake off the horrific events of the previous hours, including the scene in Jack's kitchen. Blake kept eyeballing Jack as if he would just as soon strangle him as stand there and talk. Rob and Jack had carried the conversation, catching up, relaxed and ignoring Blake's angry stare. He had kept an arm around Sara, unwilling to let her go, after yet another tongue lashing about "bad choices." She let him hold her. He was a control freak but had always watched out for her. It was soothing to lean against him even though he was staring daggers at Jack.

At one point her body starting shaking so badly she nearly fell. "Excuse me, but I need to get her settled." Jack took her elbow, guiding out from under her brother's arm and made her sit, handing her a healthy pour of bourbon. She would not meet Blake's eyes, especially after Jack's pointedly possessive statement. Crouching down to be at her eye level, he ran a finger down her cheek, catching a tear that fell.

"Drink this. Then take a shower." He stood, his hand on her shoulder. "I've gotta go back in there and convince your brother I'm not Ted Bundy or worse." She smiled up at him.

"Sorry," she said and Jack shrugged.

"I've got a sister too. I know how he feels. I wouldn't let her within a country mile of me either." He leaned down to brush her lips with his. Sara's heart stuttered in her chest. A sister? There was so much she did not know about him. "Use the shower upstairs, to the left of the steps in the big bedroom. Towels are in the cabinet."

She'd gulped down the burning liquid, closed her eyes a minute, and then headed upstairs. Sara couldn't help but peek her head into the other three upstairs rooms. One was as a home office, with a huge television screen and enormous desk complete with large flat monitor and keyboard. The other two were bedrooms, tastefully minimal. Jack's room was gigantic, a real man-space with a dark walnut king-sized bed, a closet as big as her bedroom, and a bathroom fit for a resort spa. Sara ran a hand across the marble vanity top before slipping out of her clothes and into a thick robe she found hanging on the door. Pulling the thick plush fabric to her nose, she took in a huge breath of Jack's scent before turning on all six of the shower heads on full force, full hot.

She could hear the low bass notes of masculine conversation. The occasional laugh made her hope against hope that her brother was thawing a little. She let the hot water rinse the soapy foam off her body, determined to ignore the weird situation she'd found herself. Images crashed in on her. Flashes of terror and pain invaded, the man's ugly sneer when he hit her, the sensation of his nasty body pressed against hers. She braced herself on the tiled wall and tried not to panic. The water suddenly stopped.

"Hey," she whirled around to find Jack holding a huge thick towel, a smile on his face.

She stepped into his embrace; let him dry her off, head to toe. He ended with her hair, rubbing it between the folds of absorbent fabric, his face close to hers, not speaking. She could hear music playing somewhere. Dropping the towel to the floor between them he cradled her face between his hands, kissed her forehead, her nose, and finally her lips, soft at first, then with more intensity, his tongue invading her mouth, owning her, making her gasp for breath.

"Jack," she started, breaking away. "I should..." he cut her off with another kiss, pulling the robe around her shoulders again.

"You should stay here with me, tonight," he muttered into her wet hair. "Let me take care of you. I don't want you out of my sight, ever, although I realize the impracticality of that."

She melted at that and cursed her eyes for leaking even more tears, wrapped her arms around his neck, going up on tiptoe to reach his lips. Jack scooped her up, carried her to his bed, and held her until she fell into a deep sleep. Sara didn't even realize how bone-tired she was until her head was nestled against his shoulder.

Sara jerked awake, a scream on her lips, gasping for breath, unable to process where she was. Jack sat up next to her, soothing, pulling her back down, and covering her face with kisses. She took a deep breath and laid back, as the day came back to her. Jack's lips distracted her, moving down to her nipples, as he positioned himself between her legs in one movement. The robe she'd been wearing fell open as Jack's hands moved down her sides, to her waist and hips, as he moved from one nipple to the other, licking and sucking. Sara arched her back.

"Jack," she whispered.

"Hmm?" his mouth never left her flesh.

"Please, I…" Sara was determined to get control of this, she had to tell him how she felt but felt her throat closing up with familiar fear.

"What do you want me to do baby," he whispered. "Tell me."

Sara's heart pounded. This was a twist. The sensation of his hands and lips, his soft words, being here, in his bed, overwhelmed her.

"I want you to listen to me," she insisted. His lips returned to their travels down her torso; licking and kissing making her skin break out in goose bumps.

"I'm listening," he insisted. "I can multitask."

She sucked in a breath when his lips reached her clit, his tongue flicking it, his hands cupping her ass raising her up to his lips. She threaded her hands in his hair.

"Oh, God," she gave in to him, words escaping into a whirlwind of pleasure.

He sucked on her hard nub of flesh, and slipped fingers into her dripping pussy, drawing them out slowly, before reinserting, and reaching up beneath her pubic bone, making her cry out.

Jack pulled away as Sara's body pulsed and shuddered. She opened her eyes and looked at him up on his knees, amazing thick cock in his hand, staring at her, dark blue eyes unreadable. Sara stretched, her body a blaze of post-orgasmic bliss.

"What was it you wanted to say," he growled.

"That I think I…." Sara stopped, swallowing the words, rendered speechless by the sight of him, the sheer chemical connection between them undeniable. "I love…how you make me feel."

He smiled as he rubbed a hand up and down his length. Sara took a deep breath and let the words loose, self-preservation be damned. Her voice was barely a whisper.

"I love you Jack." He dropped down and tugged her arms over her head, pinning them there, making her whole body sing with response to this small gesture. His lips hovered over hers. She shut her eyes, waiting for the inevitable smart-ass remark or equally flippant response, hating herself for admitting it. "I shouldn't, but I do, and I probably shouldn't have said it either," he cut her off, his lips on hers. He kept his body separate, their lips and his hands on her wrists the only connection. When he broke away, he shifted the hand holding her down, threaded his fingers through hers and gripped hard. The tenderness in his gaze forced her to look away.

"I need this, so badly. I need you, here with me. I need to be inside you now." He gave her hand one last squeeze and reached over for a condom, stretching it down over his shaft, his eyes never leaving hers. He positioned himself between her legs, easing the head of his cock inside her. She cried out as he entered her in one long glorious stroke, stretching her, making her raise her hips and wrap her legs around his waist.

"God help me Sara," he said, his cock buried deep inside her, his pubic bone pressed against her still throbbing clit. "I love..." She used her muscles to grip along his thick shaft. He gritted his teeth, and Sara smiled up at him.

"Tell me Jack. I need to hear it."

"I want….ahhh, God, woman," he pounded into her, hard, making her reach up and grip the smooth wood headboard to match his thrusts. She shut her eyes, letting the orgasm take her, as he grunted and came, crying out with her. Their bodies stayed connected, as she wrapped her arms around his head. "I love you." He mumbled into her damp skin. "And God help me just as much."

He pulled out and collapsed down beside her. She took a deep breath and turned to him.

"Don't hurt me Jack," she warned, putting a finger to his lips. "I may love you but I won't put up with bullshit." He grinned and put the tip of her finger in his mouth.

"Are you kidding? Your brother scares the living shit of me. Now flip over, we need our beauty sleep."

Sara grinned, and snuggled into his body, letting him spoon her. Her brain spun so fast she wondered how she'd get to sleep, but her body calmed, satisfied, and finally truly content she drifted off in Jack's arms.

The next morning Sara woke, stretched and rolled over to find the bed empty. She rose, wrapping the robe back around her, crept out into the quiet hallway.

"Jack," she called down the steps. Silence greeted her. The dim early morning light flooded the hall from a bank of large windows. She found the coffee maker, figured out where he kept all the supplies and marveled at the extreme neatness and organization of his kitchen as she assembled a pot. He'd left his phone on the counter, and it buzzed at least twice while she was standing there, staring out the window, unable to process the fact that Jack Gordon had actually said that he loved her. She was close to admitting that the entire thing terrified her to the point of jumping in her car and escaping until she realized her car wasn't here.

At the next buzz of the phone, she picked it up, realizing too late her mistake. Three messages from "Heather" popped up.

"Hey, we still on for tonight?"

"I'm getting in the shower, I'll be thinking about you and our last shower together."

And finally, the showstopper:
"Call me lover. I miss you. I need you. I love you."

Sara was cold and hot all at once. Her natural tendency to compartmentalize, to shove anything resembling real emotion aside in a self-preserving reflex, had failed her. She'd opened up. She had admitted the worst possible thing to the worst possible man on the planet. She set the phone down, resisting the urge to hurl it against the wall. Sun pierced the fog outside, hitting her square in the face. With it came the hard realization that Jack was indeed going to hurt her and she had nothing to blame but her own weakness.

She spotted her own phone next to the chair where she'd sat last night, snatched it up and called Blake.

"Come get me," she spat out. "I'm still…"

"I'll be there in fifteen," he cut her off. Running upstairs to find her clothes, she started to pull them on and then tossed the ripped shirt into the bin in Jack's over the top bathroom, tears blinding her as she reached into one of his dresser drawers for a replacement. She pulled the first t-shirt she found over her head, and ran back downstairs. She heard the door slam and Jack's voice.

"Smells good in here," he called. She scowled at the sound and walked into the kitchen. His large torso gleamed with a sheen of sweat from his run.

"Hey," he turned and tried to pull her into an embrace. She ducked to the side.

"Gotta go," she said, unwilling to engage in any level of conversation with him, unsure what she might say. She glared at his confused look. He stepped back and crossed his arms over his chest still heaving with exertion.

"So soon?" His voice was non-committal.

Infuriated beyond reason, Sara turned to him.

"Yeah, *lover*," she spat out. "Sounds like you should rest up for tonight."

His brow furrowed in confusion he followed her gaze to the phone at his elbow. Grabbing it, he stared at the screen and rolled his eyes.

"Oh shit, honey, this woman is like a stalker." Sara held up a hand.

"Don't bullshit me you ass," Sara insisted. "It insults me."

"I'm not bullshitting you Sara," he insisted, his eyes darkening. "But I guess since you're used to being right, you won't believe me so," he turned and pulled a coffee mug out of the cabinet, his stance nonchalant. She stared at his broad back and resisted the extreme urge to wrap around him, cover him with kisses and forgive. Old Sara held her back, kept her distant, kept her angry.

He sipped his coffee, not speaking. Sara raised her chin at him, about to say something, anything to recover what she thought she had with him, but when Blake's horn sounded outside it brought it all back. All the rumors, the innuendo about him, her own stupid thinking she'd had any effect on him beyond physical. When would she learn? Letting her body lead, letting him control her, it was all so lame. She turned on her heel and left without saying another word, slamming the heavy front door behind and flopping into Blake's car, tears squeezing from her eyes.

"Don't talk." she gritted her teeth at her brother. "Get me to my car and away from here," she looked up to see Jack standing in the doorway, coffee still in hand, staring at her.

Her brother pulled out of the long driveway and drove her home, where her car waited, like yesterday and all its extreme drama had never happened. Blake kept a hand on her clenched fist, his touch warming and comforting.

Walking back through her own door had been a relief – more so than she thought it would be. After an hour-long soak in the tub she emerged, revitalized, and reached for her phone anticipating a message from Jack but saw nothing on her screen. Disappointed in her own need to hear from him, she fielded a call from Blake. He did his usual big brother fussing over her, scolding her for staying at Jack's, reminding her she shouldn't consider him a "boyfriend" in any sense of the word, and invited her over for dinner. She smiled but put him off, wanting some time to herself.

She lay down and slept on the couch for most of the day, her body still processing the extremes of the previous forty-eight hours. When she awoke her mouth dry and empty stomach rumbling her phone buzzed with a call.

"Sara," Craig's voice was as soft and soothing as she remembered.

"Hey you," she curled up on the couch.

"You home?"

"Yeah," she twirled a lock of damp hair around her finger. "I just slept the entire day away. I'm starving" Talking to her rescuer made some of the residual anger and frustration with Jack fade ever so slightly.

"Funny you should mention that. I happen to have a spare peach pie with me."

Sara sat up straighter.

"Peach pie? That's my favorite," she smiled at the coincidence but had to wonder why the hell a grown single man would have a "spare" peach pie on him.

"Yeah, I know," he said. "And if you'll open your door, I can hand it to you."

She jumped up and pulled the door open to find a smiling blond man, clad in plaid shorts and soft white plain t-shirt, closing his phone and holding a boxed pie imprinted with Blake and Rob's restaurant logo. She rolled her eyes and leaned on the doorjamb, appreciating the young, fit and tanned vision in front of her.

"And here I thought you went and baked for me," she motioned for him to enter.

He shrugged and walked over to her kitchen placing the pie on the counter.

"All I know is I've been smelling this thing for the last fifteen minutes and have got to have some or I will kill somebody." He leaned on the counter and looked at her, his loose-limbed stance sexy and comforting all at the same time. She pushed him aside so she could reach for plates and forks and encountered that just-washed smell on him. It brought Saturday's drama crashing back to the forefront of her brain.

The kitchen walls closed in on her and she felt the jerk's hand ripping her shirt, smelled his stink, then, Jack's words, face and body, owning her, making her admit things she shouldn't have. She let out a sob.

Craig put an arm around her waist. "Hey, you okay?" She turned to him and he held her close as her body shook. He ran his hand down to the small of back which had a direct effect on her state of mind. She relaxed into his touch and reached out to grasp his shirt with both hands to hold herself upright. He was not an exceptionally tall man, and she liked how she could fit herself against him.

His lips grazed her ear. "Shhh, it's fine, relax." He continued to knead her lower back, his hands circling her hips and Sara was mortified to feel her nipples harden. Images of Jack rose in her brain and she started to pull away, letting go of the fabric that she'd bunched up between her hands.

Craig kept her close, and she let herself be held, arms curled between them, head turned to face his neck. *God he smelled so clean*. She closed her eyes but opened them in surprise when lips covered hers.

"Mmmph," she started to pull her head away and speak, but Craig put a hand under her hair and held her in place. His impossibly soft and full lips firm, his tongue caressed her, was gentle yet confident. He made a noise in his throat and pulled away.

"Sara, I'm sorry," his hoarse voice stayed low. "I," he kissed her exposed collarbone and she leaned her head back. Her nipples pressed against the worn felt of her robe. "Oh hell, I didn't mean to make this more complicated." He let go of her.

Sara held her elbows, suddenly cold and shivering. The doorbell rang, making her nearly jump out of her skin. She took one last look at him standing there, hands on hips, head bent, avoiding her eyes, before she turned to take the few steps to her front door. She glanced out the peephole to see her friends Val and Cathy, brandishing a pizza and a bottle of wine. She pulled her robe together, took a deep breath and opened the door. They burst in, made their familiar way to her kitchen and stopped dead at the sight of their latest office heartthrob holding a plate of pie, keeping himself behind the tall counter Sara knew to disguise the evidence of their near encounter. She grinned to herself but stopped.

Why the hell are you playing with him, Sara? New Sara chided her. *He is not what you want. Don't use him to cover what you really need – Jack. Back in your arms.*

The girls popped open the wine and started pouring everyone a glass but Craig put his plate in the sink and begged off, giving Sara a chaste hug on his way out. She followed him to the door. As he was going to take the single step down to the sidewalk, he turned, walked back up to her, pulled her out onto the tiny front step and planted a firm kiss on her lips, one arm around her waist. He ended the kiss before she could wrap herself around him. "I'm actually not sorry," he said. "Can I call you?" She nodded, stunned and quivering and watched him fire up his ten year old SUV and screech out of the parking lot. She pulled her hair up off her neck and sighed. The girls had piled in behind her and were staring, open mouthed.

"What," she asked them as she breezed past back into her home.

"No fair, Sara," Cathy complained before they clinked glasses. "You get both Stewart hot guys?" Sara rolled her eyes.

Apparently, she did. Now what?

CHAPTER ELEVEN

The next few days were a blur of business and gut-churning denial for Jack. The urges he'd resisted for years, the need to control and dominate, to be responsible for the emotional and physical satisfaction of a woman roared through him, coloring his every waking and sleeping moment. Sitting down and writing out in an email to Sara how sorry he was and explaining away Heather's texts the day she'd left, had gotten him some forgiveness, at least online, but he hadn't actually seen Sara since. He was sick with worry after what she'd been through. He needed her to need him. Yet he left her alone, thinking that was best for someone as strong-minded as Sara. But it sucked; every single minute of it.

"Jack." He tore his eyes from the computer screen and focused on his assistant.

"What." He stood, stretched, felt the pleasant soreness in his limbs from a punishing ten-mile run earlier and let Jason walk him through the next couple of days. He zoned at one point, completely unlike him, but unable to stop images of her eyes, her ass offered to him, her down on her knees in front of him.

"Yo! Dude!" Jason snapped his fingers. "Stay with me, there's a lot going on."

"Nope, sorry, I'm no use to anybody today." Jack grabbed his suit jacket from the chair and pulled it on. "Send me an email with all details. I gotta get out of here." He breezed past agents, secretaries and others. His vision had darkened, tunneled, and he knew if he didn't get out he'd rip into somebody who didn't deserve it, or worse.

Without thinking about it, he found himself at Evan and Suzanne's brewery, sitting in the car, trying to catch his breath. Closing his hand around his phone, he bit down on the urge to call her, to reach out somehow. No. She needed to come to him this time.

He took a seat in the already busy tap room, not meeting anyone's eyes, unwilling to engage in conversation other than the one he came here to have. Suzanne brought him a beer without a word, sensing his need for quiet. Evan emerged from the brewery, wiping his hands on a towel and tossing instructions over his shoulder. His smile widened at the sight of his friend. Jack raised his glass to him.

"What brings you here on a Wednesday?" Evan grabbed a glass and leaned across the bar.

"I need you to tell me I'm not losing my mind."

"Huh." Evan grinned at him. "Need me to help you put on your makeup too? How about adjust your tampon."

"Fuck. You."

"No. Thanks."

Jack knocked back the rest of his beer and pushed the glass at his friend. "What are you standing there for? Serve me." Evan raised an eyebrow then turned and refilled the glass with the amber hoppy brew Jack liked. "You just blew your tip." Even flipped him off with a smile.

"You are not losing your mind. You're just readjusting. I know. It was tough for me too."

"Whatever, man, it is killing me." He shifted, trying to release the skin-crawling sensation he'd sustained for four days. Four days of not seeing her, not even talking beyond some email and text exchanges while she "worked out" how she felt about him. "I'm obviously no good at this. I told you that the last time." Evan rolled his eyes. A soft feminine hand on his shoulder made Jack jump and nearly spill his beer.

"Dude, relax." Evan smiled over his shoulder, and Jack saw his face settle into familiar lines, happy ones. "She won't bite. Well, unless you want her to."

Jack smiled at the stunning blonde woman who'd captured Evan's heart, kissed her lightly on the lips and looked back at his friend. "Dude," he emphasized the word. "You let this gorgeous creature out in broad daylight for anyone to see? I mean, really. I'm disappointed in you."

Julie's laugh was light. "Yeah, keeps him on his toes." She accepted a glass of deep brown lager. Evan brushed his fingers across her lips before leaning back over to Jack. Suddenly struck deep by the bond between them Jack couldn't tear his eyes away. It was as if he could actually see it, a thin, strong strip of light from Evan's hand to her. He shook his head. Damn, next thing he'd know he'd be crying and would need a tampon adjustment.

As Julie leaned back on her bar chair, Jack saw it. Around her neck. Just a flash of metal he knew would be platinum, forged with a single connection that took a small key to release. He sucked in a breath, visions of Sara again bombarding him, her wearing his collar, his ring, anything, to prove she was his. He ran a hand down his face, suddenly exhausted.

"You have to let it happen. Otherwise, it will eat you alive. I can tell it already is. It's who you are – who *we* are. You've been denying yourself this for too long." Evan's low voice spoke the truth he needed to hear. Jack looked up at the ceiling.

"You're right. But…" Evan held up a hand.

"No. No excuses."

"Fine." He stared to rise, feeling trapped again, claustrophobic, and bone tired.

"We're going to the club this weekend." Evan nodded at Julie. "I think you should come."

"I don't know, man."

"I do. But can you get Sara to come too? Even if you can't, you should join us. I really think it will help you."

His phone buzzed with a text at that second. He glanced at it and he felt his vision darken slightly at the sight of Sara's name. *Mine.*

"Speak of the devil." He sat back down. "But no, she isn't ready for that. Especially, not after what happened to her last weekend."

"Yeah, you may be right. But the invite stands." Jack watched as Evan and Julie exchanged a silent bit of communication. Julie was a fiercely independent woman – a successful in her own right. It really proved what he'd always known. A true submissive had to be strong in order for the relationship to thrive. Choosing to submit took strength. A weak-willed personality, who wanted nothing but to be topped day and night, did not lead to success in a situation where so much depended on the meshing of two personalities. He sighed. Jenna, in a nutshell. Weak-willed while pretending to be strong. It had been her fault, but also his as he'd been young and untested, just going with his natural rookie instincts.

"*Hey*" he stared at the single word she'd sent, realizing it spoke volumes about where she was in her head regarding him. He smiled and typed.

"Is your pussy bare and ready for me?'

Sara grinned at Jack's text in spite of herself. "*Busy*" she shot back.

"Big Deal. I'm having a beer but thinking of you and your bare pussy – multitask with me"

She waited about thirty minutes before sending back: "*Well my bare pussy and I are about to sell a million-dollar house so there.*"

"Cool. Remember, don't push. Million-dollar buyers need more hand holding than you think.

After an hour, she got a new text.

"What are you wearing?"

She really was trying to show these houses and get one sold, but could not help but smile as she responded while her buyers traversed the current gargantuan house.

"Skirt, blouse, shoes, you know the usual"

"No, underneath"

"Nothing, except a sheer bra"

"Nice. Just the picture I needed to get me through the rest of the day."

Sara carried on until about five p.m., when she was with another set of buyers before her phone alerted her to another text: *"I want to lick your nipples."*

Her scalp tingled.

"Might be awkward right now, with people"

"Let em watch – something tells me you'd like that as much I would."

The email he had sent her the night after she'd bolted from his house, explaining away the "Heather texts" again, reminding her that he was new to the "relationship thing," had gone a long way towards melting the ice forming around her heart. Telling her he meant what he'd said, but that he thought they both needed to "take it slow" was something she could relate to, especially since he was the one to say it first. She'd kept reading about the lifestyle Jack had once lived. Realized they were a nearly perfect fit. She was willing, practically compelled to submit to him. Something in her psyche needed it. But it was so far outside the realm of her reality, she needed more time to adjust. She sensed he was easing back into something very powerful, something he needed to re-learn how to control.

His email had been long, eloquent, and heartfelt. She'd read it about a hundred times before responding. They'd engaged in a long back and forth that night and, Sara believed, had worked through some stuff.

She frowned, waiting for the intolerable buyers to finish wasting her time. Craig had been ignoring her for the bulk of the week, avoiding her eyes when they passed each other in the hall, asking for advice from other agents instead of her, like he used to. She was conflicted, aggravated at them both and herself.

A final message, around six pm:

"Hey, you going to this thing your brother is hosting out on Strawberry Lake or wherever?"

She reddened, but was not that surprised he knew about it. She would have given anything to stroll into the party on Jack's arm, his attention only for her, and have her brother accept it.

Fat chance, on both counts.

After the heartfelt email, he hadn't ignored her or anything, but seemed unwilling to revisit the conversation. It made her nuts, this not knowing, but she reminded herself she should take what she could get from him, and what she wanted more than anything right now, was his hands on her body.

Funny, this addiction to him. No, not funny. Fucking annoying.

"Of course. He invited you? Really?"

"Sure. I'm the life of any party"

"Whatever. I'll be there."

"Wanna ride – I can show you my new wheels."

"I guess – not sure I'm safe with you though."

"You're as safe as you want to be Sara"

"Pick me up in half an hour, my place"

He showed up in an amazing 1962 Lincoln Continental convertible, red, with a white leather interior. It was all she could do not to laugh out loud.

"Jesus, Jack, seriously," she asked as she walked toward the passenger side to let herself in. Her every nerve ending was tingling; New Sara could not wait to be near him again. The little homey, domestic scenarios that had played through her waking thoughts kept intruding. Would it be possible for them to ever take things a step further? She didn't know after her extreme reaction to that girl's text messages. She didn't know if her psyche could take it. Did she even want it? Her brother kept pressing her to go out with Craig – an officially Blake-approved mate.

She slid into her seat, leaned her head back and sighed. The decision suddenly appeared, bright and clear. She'd tell him once more. Give him a chance to accept or retreat. The word "trust" had to play a big part in the conversation whether he liked it or not.

"Nice car," she said, not looking at him. The radio had been replaced at some astronomical expense with a modern, satellite version, and old 80s college rock poured from the speakers as he held his arm over the bench seat back and grinned at her.

"Thanks, I like it." He grabbed a beer for her and himself a bottle of water from a cooler in the back seat.

Sara had managed to persuade two different buyers to meet her tomorrow to write offers, and strong-armed a couple of sellers into price reductions. She felt strong, determined to take back the reins of this thing with Jack, not let him hurt her but willing to open up a little again, if he would. She accepted the beer he offered and drained half of it.

It was a two hour drive out to her parent's property, which consisted of one small house with three bedrooms right on a lake and one smaller house with a room plus a bathroom they had always used for overflow guests in the summers she spent out here. Jack had great music on, the weather was perfect, and his arm stayed casually draped around her shoulders as they sang along with the Smithereens, The Clash, the Ramones and the Stones.

As they exited the freeway and began the forty-five minute drive out to the lake, she began to squirm, nervous at the thought of strolling into Blake's party with this man. The one he'd warned her about, rescued her from. Jack's hand stroked her neck, transferred to her thigh, moving her dress skirt up to allow him better access.

It set off a small fire in her belly but also tipped the scales in favor of what she planned to say to him today. She smiled but her throat clenched at the sight of his grin and moved his hand off her leg and back onto the steering wheel.

"Pull over at the first left," she held her hands together, fighting the urge to touch him. She had to have her say. Whenever she was this near Jack something in her knew they were a great fit. Her heart lifted at the thought of their night together, the day of her attack, giving her strength. He did as she said, and made his way into a small open space about a quarter of a mile from the road, private and surrounded by tall trees.

"Hey," he said, turning to her. "Did you lose your virginity here?"

"Maybe." She shifted in her seat and turned to face him as he shut off the engine. "Wait." She dodged the hand he extended to pull her close.

"Okay." He sat back, his eyes darkening. There was a palpable change in the air and Sara gulped once, trying like hell not to lose her nerve.

"I, um, want to talk. Really talk just a minute. I mean, I think that we have potential. I'm not averse to the lifestyle you have, ah, introduced me to. It's not that. I'm just afraid,"

"Sara, we've been through this."

"No, let me finish." She bit her lip and forced herself to continue. "I think I could be this…this…submissive for you. I think I might even like it but, from what I've read about this arrangement trust is a key component."

"Yes, it is." His eyes narrowed, his long finger tapped against the back of the leather seat, distracting her.

"Well, the thing is, Jack, I don't know that I can. Trust you that is. I don't think you are ready to let me. No." She held up a hand against his protest. "I have more. It's okay. I mean, I wish I could but I have to be honest with myself and engage a little self-protection here, you know?"

He blew out a breath and looked up at the dark green canopy that covered them. "But what if I say I'm willing to try? That you make me want to trust and be trustworthy more than any human being I've ever met?" Sara sucked in a breath. This wasn't what she'd expected. Something along the lines of, "You're right babe. Now let's fuck some more," or something like that would have been more in keeping with the mental conversations she'd had with him in the last few days.

"I'd say that is admirable." She simply could not resist putting a hand against his darkened cheek. "But is it realistic?"

He wouldn't meet her eyes. She leaned back, hands clenched tight in her lap. "I would do it you know. I'd live this way with you. It makes me happy, content, turned on, all the stuff it's supposed to do. But," she gasped when he gripped her arms, hauled her up and onto his lap, his lips covering hers, his hands fisted in her hair. She straddled him, felt his need press against her. He finally broke the lip lock.

"I have a different proposal for you." She raised an eyebrow at him, her body on fire, her mind equally ablaze.

"How about you let me prove it? Give me as much as you can, small increments of trust. I need to show you I can do it. I swear," he broke away. She put her hands on either side of his face and swore, for a minute, she saw deep sadness in his eyes. Her stomach fluttered.

He reached for her then, cupped a hand behind her neck and covered her protests with a kiss that made her doubt anything and everything she had said to him. She tore her lips away with some effort, put her hands on his shoulders and glared at him.

"A trial period, eh? For how long? I'm a busy girl. Gotta schedule things."

He grinned and cupped a breast under her dress. "Control freak." He moved her strap aside, leaned into suck a nipple into his mouth. She threaded her fingers in his hair, her heart singing with happiness.

"Yeah, give it a deadline. You know, in case I need to keep my options open."

He released her nipple, gripped her hair harder, making her gasp with the pleasure/pain sensation so much a part of her relationship with him so far. His normally low, growly voice went down an octave, making her shiver all over. "You don't need any other option baby. I've got everything you need." She nodded, speechless. This was going to work.

"I need you," she heard New Sara tell him. He reached for her, but she forced his hands back. Readjusting herself on her knees, she reached in and grabbed his neck, pulling his face to her, demanding a kiss. He gave her want she wanted, yanked her dress up to gain access to her bare pussy and ass. Without another word, she unzipped his shorts and gripped him, making him sigh with pleasure. "Hang on, I brought protection." She smiled and showed him the condom she'd retrieved from her purse.

"So, Sara is a girl scout," he muttered, closing his eyes as she rolled the thin sheath down his shaft.

"Yeah a girl learns how to take care of herself." His cock was so hard it pressed up tight against his lower belly. She straddled him, allowed herself only minimal penetration. She dipped her pussy onto the thick head of his cock, took one of his hands and guided it to her nipple, which was nearly exploding with anticipation.

"Wait." He held her hips, not letting her envelop him fully. "You have to understand something. This is your choice. Something you can take away anytime. But…" he sighed, releasing her so she could take him into herself, as they both groaned at the sensation. He tugged her chin down, making her meet his eyes. "You scare me Sara. The way I feel about you terrifies me. And when I get scared I act stupid, fair warning."

She reacted to his voice like an animal, her skin flushed, her clit sensitized in way that made her nearly mad with need. She wanted him – all of him, all of the time, but if this was all he would give, well, she'd take it. She responded by sitting on him fully, taking his thickness all of the way inside her, and gasped from the familiar stretching sensation.

His hands grasped her hips, forced her back up. He looked at her a moment, his gaze puzzled, but New Sara ignored his confusion and lowered herself back down, taking him into her fully, again and again. She closed her eyes and let it happen, felt her orgasm roaring up with every penetration. She shoved his shirt up and ran her hands across his incredibly sculpted upper body. Consciously tightening her vaginal muscles, she watched his eyes, aware of the response she would get.

"Don't be stupid Jack." She whispered, nearly breathless. "You can trust me, too."

When he reached around and grabbed her ass with both hands, and brought his lips back to her nipple she tipped over the edge, moaning and crying out his name as the orgasm embraced her. She brought his face up to hers; wanting to kiss his lips, share it with him. She continued to flex her inner muscles and raise herself up and down on Jack's magnificent cock, as he reached his own climax, groaning into her mouth.

She remained in place a few minutes, trying to restore her normal breathing pattern. He sighed into her neck. "Okay," he muttered, "I think I've been used and abused, but I liked it," He shifted as she lifted herself off him.

She laughed. "Let's go, the party's started. Might as well face Blake now. That's part of my deal. He has to know."

Jack groaned. "Okay but try to keep him from throttling me, will ya?" She leaned over to kiss him, her body sated, her mind clear.

They reached the cabin, its lights ablaze, music pouring out of all windows, people inside and out. Jack started out with his arm around her shoulders, but released her. She figured he was going to grab drinks for them and started across the room to talk with a friend. When she caught sight of an extremely tall and exotic looking woman making a beeline for him, she blinked, still in a slight stupor from her recent orgasm. Her eyes narrowed as the woman whispered something in Jack's ear, making him frown. *Heather*. It had to be. She swallowed hard.

Trust him Sara. You have to give him a chance. He's probably telling her to back off.

She walked up to Blake who stood at the grill turning hamburgers.

"Hey sister." He glared over at Jack then leaned in to whisper into her ear, "You smell like sex. What the hell is he doing here?"

"Hey Blake," she put her arm around his wide shoulders. "He's, ah, my date." The sudden feel of something cold against her arm made her squeal. She jumped and turned, fully expecting Jack to be standing there with a cold one for her. When she looked straight into Craig's deep chocolate eyes her skin prickled. He smiled at her, and held out the sweating brown bottle. She closed her eyes, trying to tamp out the distinct sound of Jack's laughter drifting across the room. She opened an eye, took the bottle, emptying half in one drink.

Blake shook Craig's hand, and Sara looked around the room pretending not to notice Jack and the woman he claimed was a stalker. As if sensing her glare, Jack turned his head, winked at her, and then turned the full force of his attention to the woman practically panting in front of him. She kept touching his arm, his chest, but to his credit, he would remove her hand whenever it reached him. Sara clutched the bottle tighter, finished it off, and put the empty down before stomping away.

Trust goddamn it. Why was he making so hard?

Sara greeted some friends on her way to the beer coolers, grabbed another one, stood and opened it as she turned. Craig stood at the other end of the long table filled with food, laughing with Jen, the admin girl he'd been linked with through company gossip. Sara's face flushed.

She attempted to locate Jack without looking around too obviously. Her second beer went down quickly, and she made her way over to Rob, ignoring Craig as she passed him.

"Hey," her brother's handsome lover said his back to her as he turned the shrimp and chicken kabobs on the massive grill.

"Don't," she demanded. "Just...don't, okay?"

"You said yourself it was only physical," he muttered to her. "Why do you expect him to act any different?"

"You know what," she hissed at him, "You don't know the whole story. We are together for your information and he has to tell her that," she nodded over to where Jack and Heather had been standing. They were nowhere in sight. She gulped and clenched her fists as Rob put a hand on her shoulder.

Needing space from him and his unspoken "I told you so", she made her wobbly way across the large deck to her friends. Passing by an open door, she heard Jack's low laughter – the sound of him in full on seduction mode was hard to miss since she'd been on the receiving end of it so frequently.

While her brain screeched at her to keep walking, to ignore what she heard, her feet led so she found herself in the gloomy main room of the cabin. She kept walking until she was in the doorway out to the back deck. The overgrown wisteria vines provided dim corners perfect for secret trysts as Sara well knew from years of experience. The sound of a woman's giggle and the distinct and recognizable noise of a kiss froze her in place. She sucked in a deep breath and stepped out onto the deck.

"Jack," she heard a woman's high-pitched voice stretching his name out to several syllables. "I thought you had forgotten about me." The woman giggled again, an annoying nails on a chalkboard sound to Sara's rattled brain.

"No, no. Now, now hang on. I'm here with someone. Cool your jets." Sara stood and listened, willing to hear his side of the conversation. "Listen, Heather, I'm not…I mean I think I'm, whoa hands off sweetheart." Sara heard the woman whimper.

"Hang on, aren't you gonna finish what you started?" Heather's voice got breathier. "I mean, you found me at this thing even though you came with. . ." Jack cut her off.

"Actually you found me. Look, I gotta get back. Sorry but you can't, oh hell, seriously, stop it." He groaned, making the hairs on the back of Sara's neck stand up.

Mine.

The woman made a disappointed, whiny sound. Sara finished off the beer and set the bottle down with a clunk, alerting the asshole and the slut with him to her presence.

There was more rustling and a feminine squeal. She took another step out into the sunlight and saw Jack sitting with Heather half draped over his lap. She turned her head and glared at Sara, putting a blatant hand on Jack's crotch. He shot up, knocking her to the floor, watching Sara the entire time.

Some combination of post Jack-induced orgasm stupor and extreme anger at his bullshit attitude since they hit the party made her body thrum with fury but she forced herself to get real. God, she should know better by now. The guy was nothing but a walking hard on, apparently, without any scruples or emotion whatsoever. His stupid email excuses, and her own willingness to let it slide these past days collided in her brain. She would never, ever trust him, no matter how badly she wanted to. It invited heartbreak and disaster, two things she had no time for anymore.

"Sorry to interrupt," Sara put a hand on the wall to steady herself. "Don't stop on my account, Jack," she hissed at him, ignoring the woman as she sat back on the bench and tugged Jack's hand. His eyes narrowed, "Since we came together I thought you might need to know I'm leaving. You know, so you won't wonder where I am or anything." Sara whirled around before she let tears drop before turning back to him and grinding out. "By the way, your time is up."

"Wait, Sara. Christ, Heather would you please *stop*."

She picked up her pace, able to sidestep the furniture through her veil of tears since Blake hadn't changed anything from the time they used to hang here as kids. Her brother stood in the small kitchen and caught her arm as she passed by.

"Don't touch me," she yelled loud enough for the partygoers outside the front door to stop talking and stare. Blake grasped her arm anyway, and pulled her close enough to hiss into her ear.

"I didn't invite him, remember?" He put his arm around her waist. "Now calm the fuck down and don't make a scene. He doesn't deserve the attention, okay?" He pulled her close and she melted into this side, nodding her head and wiping her eyes. He gave her a tender kiss on the forehead, brushed one last tear from her cheek and propelled her ahead of him straight into Craig.

Brushing past the handsome blonde man, she marched down the steps to the large front yard, determined to get control of herself before talking to anyone else. She made it as far as the battered wooden swing her father had installed for them in the large oak tree. She grabbed the ropes in both hands, letting the tears drip onto the seat worn smooth by years of use.

I am such a fucking idiot! I do want him. I just admitted that today. He asked me to trust him and if I really thought about what he said to her out there...no. Fuck him. I won't do it.

She let go of the ropes, and sat hugging her legs, leaned against the giant tree trunk. Her head pounded with unshed tears and too much beer. A band tightened around her chest, choking her, making her mouth dry. She kicked her legs out in front of her and snorted in disgust and self-loathing. But yelped when a hand touched her shoulder.

"Sara," Craig's soft, musical voice intoned. "Hey, here, drink this," he handed her an ice-cold water bottle. She ignored him and stared straight ahead.

"Won't your date miss you," she said through clenched teeth.

"She's not my date," he slid down the tree trunk next to her, dangling his hands between his knees. She grabbed the water bottle from him and slugged half of it back, letting some spill out the side of her mouth, no longer caring how she looked. "Wanna get out of here?" He bumped against her shoulder.

She turned to him. His deep brown eyes were wide and inquiring. He shrugged.

"Or not, whatever." He studied his fingernails.

She stood, drained the water bottle and looked up on the deck filled with partiers. Her heart skipped a beat when she saw Jack stride around from behind the house, Heather scurrying after him, trying to keep up. She watched Jack's eyes scan the crowd, land on his friends Evan and Suzanne, but not walking towards them. He kept looking around, ignoring the woman standing next to him trying to talk until she threw up her hands and walked away. Sara smiled coldly. She turned to Craig.

"Yes, please, get me out of here." She put a hand on his chest, and was satisfied to hear his breath quicken at her sudden, unexpected touch. He grinned and took her hand, guiding her towards his motorcycle. She pulled back, then shrugged.

Why the hell not?

As she threaded her arm through Craig's relishing his familiar clean-washed scent a feeling of calm slipped over her zinging nerve endings.

"Sara!" she turned to see Blake on the step. "Headed out?" he yelled, louder than was necessary, Sara thought. She faced him, standing next to Craig's bike as he handed her an extra helmet.

"Yeah, thanks," she blew him a kiss, and he waved as Jack came up behind him. Sara put a helmet over her hair and Craig adjusted it under her chin. She watched as if from far away as Jack started down the steps but Blake's strong arm shot out and blocked him.

"Not today Gordon," Sara heard her brother growl. "You're lucky I don't kick your sorry ass down the steps and off my property."

She watched Jack glance down at the arm blocking his way and shoot a murderous look at her brother. Her mouth dropped open at the sight of Evan taking three long steps across the deck to stand between her brother and her lover, facing Jack, pushing him backwards. Rob had positioned himself in front of Blake who tried to follow Evan and Jack.

Craig gunned the motor so she couldn't hear anything but it was painfully obvious that Rob had some difficulty restraining Blake. The crowd stared first at him, then at Jack who had broken free of his friend's influence and was pointing at Blake. Suzanne and Evan stood on either side of him, holding his arms, until he turned and stomped off to the opposite side of the deck and out of Sara's line of sight.

Blake stood, fists clenched, neck vein popping in anger as Rob put an arm around him and led him inside. She turned, put her arms around Craig – for safety, she told herself – and laid her aching head on his shoulder as he put the bike in gear and took off down the dirt drive.

She had the distinct sensation of having ripped a huge chunk of her soul out, leaving it back on the deck when she saw how possessive the woman was with Jack.

Craig may ease that but he won't ever be what you need.

Enough! You are done with Jack Gordon. Everyone is right about him. Focus on the man who rescued you twice now – see what he has to offer instead.

Sara sighed and tried her best to force visions of Jack's face out of her head, the sight of his eyes that night when he pleaded with her to let him get close and not be afraid, that he would not hurt her.

CHAPTER TWELVE

Sweat poured off Jack's body by the time he finished an early morning ten-mile run on what promised to be a ninety-plus-degree day. He stood stooped with his hands on his knees in his front yard, surveying the street scene on the muggy Michigan early fall morning, shattered in body and mind.

"Hey Mr. Gordon," the kid across the street yelled. "Need that lawn mowed again this week?"

Jack waved at him and shook his head. "Not until it rains a little, but I'll let you know." He had a brief vision of his own father, yelling at him to get up off his ass and mow the lawn again, even after he'd mowed it a few days before. Jack had spent hours staring at the ceiling in his room vowing never, ever be the type of unrelenting, critical father his was. Now look at him, over thirty with not a kid in sight to ruin with his impossibly high expectations.

And who can you blame for that, eh, Gordon?

The thought of his own stupid behavior last week brought chills to his sweat-soaked skin and he stared up at the piercing blue sky to regain his composure. The memory of Sara's gorgeous green eyes filling with angry tears nearly seared him in half, all over again. Even though he had truly been trying to disentangle himself from Heather, she had caught them at a bad moment. Bad timing was the name of his game lately it seemed.

He turned and walked into his house – the house he'd bought with his hard-earned money, and renovated himself calling upon the years of equally hard-earned experience on the job with his father as a young man. Anymore, though, it was just an empty cavern, mocking him with its lack of a certain female presence – Sara.

The night they'd shared in his bed was never far from his mind. He'd felt so content then, better than he had in years. Had convinced himself that Sara would complete his life, could bring out his best as he coaxed out hers, and he was imagining the future with her on his run the next morning when he'd walked right into the shit storm created by his own bad behavior.

The crazy bitch, Heather, he'd picked up in his friends' beer bar would not let go of him, even though he'd only fucked her once. In a colossal fit of bad judgment, he'd reverted back to his old ways in her office at the title company a few weeks earlier. He'd attended that stupid fundraising thing with her, gotten drunk off his ass, and spent hours wishing it were Sara on his arm, even sending her texts the whole night, before passing out on Heather's couch.

She'd kept at him for days afterward, ramping up the sex talk until he'd snapped. He'd had a frustrating day, felt thoroughly avoided by Sara and had taken the woman, never once picturing any other face but Sara's the entire time. It was the stupidest thing he could have done and he was far from proud of it.

Yep, King Shit of Bad Timing Mountain, that was him.

He'd tried, wanted to be trusted. Had seen Heather at the party and decided that was the right moment to set her straight.

Jesus.

The hot shower felt great, going a long way to soothing his troubled brain. Jack let the water slide across his face, then turned to let it beat a pattern on his back as he recalled the fallout from Sara's brother's party. He and Blake had come within seconds of a brawl, and Jack knew that the man would have kicked his ass, but damned if he would let him treat his sister like some sort of precious jewel, unworthy of Jack's presence. She was a grown woman, capable of making her own decisions. Blake's over-protection had reached unreasonable proportions, something Evan and Suzanne agreed with him on, although they had both beaten him around the head and shoulders that night for his behavior even though he'd tried to explain. No one believed him. Suzanne's disappointment had been the most palpable and upsetting.

"Stop trying to prove what an asshole you are, Gordon," she'd said, her eyes bright with angry tears. "Maybe people will figure it out on their own." She'd not talked to him the rest of the night; he'd sat with Evan and stared at a baseball game until his eyes were numb with boredom. Evan had put a hand on his shoulder before he left.

"I'm going to ask Julie to marry me," he said. "But I swear on all that is holy if you don't start acting like a man and not a sex-crazed teenager, you are not gonna be invited much less stand with me. I know what you need Jack. Why you won't admit it to yourself is beyond me, but, keep acting like this and we are through. And that will piss me off so much I may even revoke your Mug Club card," he'd given Jack a fierce hug and pushed him out the door.

Jack had pondered this turn of events on the way home. Julie was a lot like Sara as best he could tell. Fiercely independent, sexy, successful, and temperamental, but Evan was not willing to lose her, jumping off the deep end in order to keep her. Going beyond a mere Dom/sub arrangement to actual marriage was a bigger leap than many realized.

Lame excuse Gordon. Listen to yourself. You want control? Then fucking take it from her. Show her how happy she can be, that she can trust you. That you can trust yourself again.

He recalled the day after the party, as he got enmeshed in work crises then had stumbled in the front door of his house to find Heather, naked, on a velvet blanket on his living room floor, candles flickering, wine open, music playing. He'd hustled her out, amid much whining and pouting. He'd tried to call Sara, text her, send her email, but she effectively ignored him. Her uncommon stubbornness made him insane, and he wanted her even more. He needed to be the caretaker, the Dominant; it suffused his every fiber. She had started to cede that to him, no matter what she said. But at that moment he wondered if they'd ever come to terms with their clashing type-A personalities. She'd struggled like hell against submission but he sensed she wanted it. He'd had plenty of practice sorting out what a submissive needed. Why couldn't he just give in and let it happen?

Jack stared at himself in the bathroom mirror. This called for a large gesture, and he was ready to make it. It was what he wanted and needed to prove it to her – in front of witnesses. He dressed, called Jason to tell him he'd be about an hour late – that he had a project he needed to complete. Once he arrived at the office, shopping trip accomplished, the two of them spent the rest of the day working on Jack's power point presentation he was giving at the Stewart all-company meeting, highlighting the progress of his downtown renovation project.

After attending two closings at the end of the day, he'd gone home, changed into running clothes and run until he'd nearly dropped from exhaustion. He'd not gone this many days without female companionship in a while and was starting to not only wet dream about Sara but daydream about her too. His many attempts to contact her still went unanswered, and the two times he'd dropped in on her office she wasn't there – or her friends were hiding her which he wouldn't doubt.

The morning of the monthly all-company meeting dawned bright and clear. Jack meant for the day to be unforgettable. He dressed in his best tailor-made blue suit, snapped his Rolex on his wrist and popped a small box into his pocket before donning sunglasses and heading out into the brain melting heat.

Jack couldn't remember a time he'd been more nervous and skipped his usual double espresso. He'd had Jason extend an invite to Blake on his behalf and was gratified to see the familiar late model F150 parked in the hotel parking lot where their meeting was held each month.

He waved to Greg Stewart as he entered the building and fielded a few work calls, working up his nerve to go in the huge room filled with milling realtors, title company minions, lenders and others. He hadn't seen Sara's car in the lot, but he knew she'd be along. She usually showed up just in time for these things. Jack took a deep breath, touched the small velvet box in his trouser pocket, pasted on his smile, and walked into the room.

Sara ran late, as usual. She'd gone to a six a.m. Bikram yoga session and made the mistake of sitting at her laptop to answer some emails before leaving the house. Caught up in a transaction crisis, she stayed sitting and typing away until nearly eight forty-five. Her phone buzzed and she glanced at the text. Craig. She smiled.

He'd been amazing during the last week after rescuing her from that fiasco of a party. They'd gone for coffee, and he had let her snivel her way through an iced latte before taking her hand across the table and telling her that he was sick of talking about Jack, and asking if she wanted to see a movie.

They'd gone to the latest summer blockbuster, shared a bucket of popcorn and she'd enjoyed the hell out of it, letting her thigh rest against his, and his arm across her shoulders. He'd not tried to kiss her or grope her or anything, but at one point she turned to catch him looking at her which made her blush and turn away.

The next night he'd asked her to go with him to his band's gig out in the Detroit suburbs. They'd taken his old SUV which smelled even more strongly of bleach. "What the hell, Craig, are you a clean freak or what," she'd insisted. He gave her an odd look.

"What, why," he asked as he steered his car into the bar's parking lot.

"Everything about you smells like bleach," she said. "And this car, it's like a swimming pool in here."

"That's because I swim every single day," he'd pulled his guitar case out of the back and opened the door for her to enter ahead of him. "How do you think I keep my boyish figure," he'd whispered in her ear, making her shiver.

She wanted him to kiss her again like he had in her condo the weekend she was attacked, but he kept his distance, treating her like a buddy. Sara didn't know if she felt relieved or annoyed by it. It was hard enough ignoring Jack's constant stream of texts, calls, and emails. She needed Craig to step up and be a real distraction. But he didn't oblige.

Three exhausting sets later, exhilarated and a little drunk from watching Craig perform, Sara waited while they broke down their equipment. The band "Jake Leg" did nineteen nineties and current rock covers. Everything from the Foo Fighters to White Stripes but also managed to sneak in a few original tunes. Singing duties alternated between Craig and his drummer. Sara couldn't remember a time she'd had more fun dancing to live music. The sight of the young man caressing the mike with his lips, his eyes squeezed shut as he riffed made her more than a little damp between the legs. She could see how women feel in love – or at least mad lust – with rock stars.

It was nearly two a.m. when they wrapped up, Craig's black t-shirt soaking wet and every female in the bar salivating and hanging around hoping to buy him a drink. Sara admired his denim-clad ass for the millionth time. She was proud of herself for going the entire three-plus hours without obsessing over Jack wondering what, or who, he was doing.

At the thought of him, his strong body, piercing blue eyes and deep voice in her ear she shuddered and squeezed her eyes shut to expel him. She opened them to find Craig pulling her to her feet.

"Hey, you still here?" He smiled and avoided the little crush of groupies that closed in on him. "Let's go, I'm starved." He propelled her ahead of him out the door.

Sara broke her hard and fast rule about eating after midnight when she smelled the amazing odors emanating from the twenty-four hour restaurant and indulged in a greasy, loaded Coney dog. At one point, as the grease dripped down her hand past her elbow, Craig reached across the table to grab her arm and pulled her fingers into his mouth. She widened her eyes at him, as the feel of his lips on her skin sent her nerve endings singing. He placed her hand on the table, face calm, and continued eating as she stared at him, not quite believing what she'd experienced.

He finished inhaling his food, wiped his mouth and moved around the booth seat so he was right next to her. She shifted, a little uneasy with the sudden close contact, keeping her eyes on her plate as he slid an arm around her shoulders., "Sorry, couldn't resist," he whispered before giving her a chaste kiss on the cheek and moving back away.

The buzz of her phone startled Sara out of her quiet shock. Jack, with his usual post-midnight text.

"You awake?"

She stared at it then raised her head to observe the blonde young man across from her, unable to process anything except her longing to have Jack's hands and lips on her. She shut the phone off resolutely and tucked it back in her back pocket.

"Jack," Craig inquired, finishing his soda.

"Who else," Sara pushed her plate away and sighed.

"You deserve better," he said, not taking his eyes from hers causing her heart to beat faster.

He is truly a lovely guy, what is your problem?

"Yeah, well, you and Blake and Rob can form a club, okay," she stood, suddenly exhausted. "But leave me out of it. I'm sick of hearing about myself."

As Craig guided her out to his truck, he kept his hand in the small of her back. She turned to him before he could open the door and put her hands on his shoulders.

"I don't want you to get the wrong idea," she started but was interrupted by a sudden onset of tears. "You are an amazing guy, and I owe you a lot, but. . . " He took a step closer, and leaned into her lips, cutting her off mid thought. Her brain buzzed as she melted into his body. His lips and tongue were insistent, forceful, pressing against and into her as her tears fell between them. She broke away, embarrassed.

He put his forehead against hers and cradled her face, running his thumbs down her cheeks. She could feel the calluses years of guitar playing had rendered on his palms and fingers.

"I'm here Sara, when you're ready," he whispered as she closed her eyes. "But not before. I have no intention of serving as a distraction, although I'm sure it would be fun." His lips touched her nose and brushed her lips as he reached behind her to open her door. She sucked in a deep breath. The chlorine scent floated out of the car and up into her head making her dizzy.

Sara sat staring at her computer screen, realizing she was going to be late to the monthly all-company meeting but frozen in place by her own ridiculous dilemma.

You don't have to fight for his attention or worry he's gonna bolt at the last minute and stick his tongue down some other girl's throat while you watch.

But he isn't what you want.

She looked at her clenched fingers in her lap, and then sighed. Grabbing her purse and phone, she ran for the car, hampered only slightly by the white pencil skirt she'd worn that day, along with the matching blouse.

She remembered feeling sorry in a superior way for those simpering agents and others who would so obviously yearn for Jack Gordon's wandering attentions.

Now look at you, Sara Jane, you are the worst one yet.

She'd effectively ignored him, his texts, calls and whatever else for over a week though, and felt stronger thanks to that and her sudden realization that the young blonde gorgeous man in her office had a crush on her.

So fuck you, Gordon, and your adoring posse. I'll see you one tall raven-haired groupie and raise you a smoking hot blonde with a guitar.

She smiled at herself in the rearview mirror, glanced at the text Craig had sent her saying he'd save her a seat, and zoomed across town. When she breezed into the large hotel conference room, her eyes were immediately drawn to the nearly six-foot woman with a sleek curtain of black hair in fuck-me pumps and a designer-style suit standing in the middle of the room. She was laughing, in an obvious "notice me" sort of way and had a well-

manicured hand on the arm of the man in front of her. *Heather.*
Great.

The room filled up, everyone eager to hear more about
Jack's downtown project. She grabbed coffee and a yogurt and
glanced around; ignoring the woman she'd caught with Jack, trying
not to see where he was at the moment when she came face to face
with Blake.

"Jesus," she declared, nearly spilling her coffee. "You
scared me."

He stood with his hands in his trouser pockets, his hair still
wet from a shower, observing her. "What?" She demanded. "Why
are you here?"

"Nice to see you too," he put an arm around her shoulders
and kissed her temple. His solid, comforting presence made her
smile in spite of herself. "I got a personal invite from Jack," he said
as he gazed around the room. Sara started and stepped away from
him. He shrugged. "His building is a block from our place so I
guess he thought I might want to know more." He waved at
someone across the room. "I'm gonna stand at the back and take off
after his little dog and pony. I'll catch you later." He gave her
shoulders another squeeze and strolled away.

Sara kept scanning the room, smiling, and chatting with a
few colleagues, on a mission to find Craig. Cathy came up behind
her and propelled her towards a middle table. "Over here Sara," she
said. We've got a spot for you." Sara let herself be guided and got a
little thrill at the sight of Craig smiling at her. He pulled a chair out
and she reddened as she sensed everyone watching. She caught
Val's smirk across the table and stuck her tongue out at her.

Greg Stewart stood at the podium and cleared his throat,
which brought some semblance of quiet to the noisy room. Sara
congratulated herself on having not looked for Jack as she peeled
the lid off her yogurt. At that moment, she heard him, his deep
laughter first then his voice.

"No, you call me when you have a real offer," he clapped
some poor woman on the shoulder and Sara watched her redden at
his touch. Her own thighs clenched and her scalp tingled but she
chided herself on her body's involuntary reaction.

Come on Sara, Jack is not all that...

She smiled weakly at Craig, not really seeing him, as New Sara whined in her ear. *Oh yes. He is. And you know it.*

The eyes of about every single female in the room followed his broad, blue wool clad shoulders as he made his way to the front, stopping to speak to a few agents but completely ignoring Heather who shot him a look of combined fury and desire. She took a deep breath, kept her back to the podium, and continued eating, trying her very best to calm her pounding heart.

Craig moved his chair a few inches nearer hers and she felt her pulse slow down. Her throat unclenched enough to swallow a few bites of un-tasted yogurt. She told herself she'd stay turned away until Jack's little show was finished. The table went quiet, and Greg greeted his agents, reviewed a few upcoming dates, including their annual fall picnic before introducing "the man who needs no introduction." The room buzzed with anticipation.

Sara rolled her eyes at Val whose eyes stayed fixed on the podium. They all waited for Jack's latest details and power point of condo floor plan options, prices and retail opportunities. She heard him thank Greg, make a joke that she couldn't hear for the buzzing in her ears. She let her gaze rest on her brother, who leaned against one of the back doors, coffee cup in one hand, eyes neutral and trained on the man he hated. Sara saw Blake frown then stand up straight his mouth hanging open as room simultaneously erupted in noise. She clenched her freezing hands in her lap, forcing herself to stay turned away from Jack and his screen.

"What the..." she heard Craig mutter and saw Val stare at the screen then at her, pointing her finger at the screen behind Sara's back. She couldn't process the noise and had no idea why everyone was so worked up. Had he flashed a naked photo of himself up there or something? She wouldn't put it past him.

The distinct sound of dozens of females sighing in unison finally made her turn. The buzzing in her ears increased as she gazed on her own name, flashed up on the screen in enormous letters. Sweat prickled her upper lip and her knees shook as the room narrowed to a tunnel connecting her eyes with the deep blue ones of the man at the podium. If it were possible to feel someone shooting daggers into her chest, she'd be dead twice over from Heather's glare.

"Sara Jane Thornton." The screen screamed in red letters. "Will You Marry Me? Jack"

By sheer instinct, she swiveled her head around to face her brother, still standing at the back of the room, mouth no longer open; dismay in his bright green eyes as he looked straight at her. She slumped back in her seat, as her face flushed red and her heart started its erratic rhythm again.

It felt like hours passed before someone tapped her shoulder. Craig, eyebrows raised in question and gaze flat, nodded towards the front of the room. She looked at him, adrenaline rushing through her veins and stood on wobbly legs. Jack had not spoken once. He stood, hands in his pockets and watched her, ignoring the buzz and clamor he had caused in the room of two-hundred-plus professionals. She glanced over her shoulder at Blake, glared at Jack, then once more at Craig who leaned back in his chair, legs stuck out in front of him, a nonchalant look fixed firmly in place.

Sara barely remembered walking the twenty feet or so up to the front, willing her heart to slow, her body to stop overreacting so she could formulate an appropriate response to his over-the-top, public proposal. Her mind and heart reeled. She felt the green monsters of nearly every female in the room pressing down on her and realized she had to walk right past Heather to reach the front. Each step brought her closer to the man she had confessed her love for a few weeks ago but whose very presence now made her want to stab him with a dull pencil.

What the fuck was he thinking, making a spectacle like this?

Her eyes burned as she kept them locked on his trying to determine if the whole thing were a dream. The sapphire blue of Jack's gaze pulled her closer. When she finally arrived in front of him, she crossed her arms and cocked her head, bringing laughter from the crowd.

Jack looked around for a split second, then pulled a velvet box from his trouser pocket, opened it and went down on one knee. The room exploded with applause, chatter and more female sighs.

Sara stood, frozen, observing what must be a four-carat emerald-shaped diamond set in platinum. Visions of Jack with Heather on his lap and the feel of Craig's strong body pressed to hers as he drove her away from that terrible party fought for attention in her brain. She met Jack's eyes again.

"Really?" she mouthed, arms still crossed.

"Yes, really," he got to his feet, took the ring out its velvet nest and held out his hand for hers.

Pushy bastard.

He pulled her close, and whispered in her ear. "You have to trust me this time. I mean it." He groaned, making her smile. "Hell I can't even do this right."

Ignoring the near silence in the room full of people she pulled back and stared at him. "Why here? What's with the big gesture? It's not fair. I feel a tad manipulated."

He grinned. "Good. That's my plan." He shut off her response with lips, firm and commanding. His tongue teased her a moment as cheers rang down around them. Sara felt her whole body lighten. Could this possibly be happening?

Sara broke the kiss, took a deep breath, placed her hand in his and nodded, as tears slipped down her cheeks. If it were possible, the room got even louder. Sara couldn't hear anything but Jack as he stood, took her in his arms, and kissed so deeply her head spun.

"You won't regret it Sara," he finally whispered. "I promise. You can trust me. I promise that too."

He took her hand, and they faced the now standing group. The fact that the words "I love you," were on her lips but unsaid did not escape her rattled brain, but there was time enough for that later. Her eyes scanned the crowd, saw that Blake had left and that Craig was the only one not standing. He sat, legs still sprawled in front of him, arm hooked over the back of his chair, staring at Sara with unasked questions in his eyes.

She wiped her wet face, smiled at her colleagues, gave Jack a peck on the cheek, and a slap on the ass to the delight of all and returned to her seat. Her face burned and the enormous diamond felt heavy on her finger.

"I'd say, 'get a room you two', but from what I understand, you don't usually require one," Greg Stewart bellowed into the microphone causing a fresh round of laughter as Sara rolled her eyes and sat not meeting Craig's look.

He leaned over to her. "Congratulations and good luck," he pressed a soft kiss on her cheek, rose and left the room. Sara squeezed her eyes shut for a second, realizing she'd likely made the sort of fork-in-the-road decision one should not make in public. She was beyond pissed at Jack for putting her in such a spot. Pats on her back and a table full of friends wanting to see her ring brought her back to the room as she stared at the gem on her left hand ring finger. Smiling at the man she had agreed to marry in front of two hundred of her nearest and dearest, and about ten or fifteen intensely jealous women, her mind spun but her heart sang as it resumed something resembling a normal rhythm.

Sara took deep breaths, let thoughts of weddings and dealing with her parents flit in and out of her head. When Jack looked straight at her during his presentation and winked she surprised herself by blowing him a kiss. Maybe this would be fine after all. Plenty of time for the "I love you's" later.

She watched as her fiancée put the final flourishes on his presentation, descended the podium, and sat in the chair Craig had vacated. He leaned into her ear. "I love you Sara. Thank you." He kissed her hand then turned around to listen to the rest of the meeting, leaving her speechless and, for the first time since laying eyes on him, truly happy.

The End...

Sweat Equity (Stewart Realty - Book 2)
Available from Sizzlin' Books

Sara sat, blanket clutched to her breasts, breathing heavy with sweat trickling down her neck. She was shocked the entire resort didn't awake from her scream. Glancing over at the sleeping man next to her, she tried to let his presence soothe as it normally did. He snored and rolled over onto his side, flinging an arm across her lap.

The tall woman from her dream would not fade. "You can't trust him Sara. Believe me. He only gave you that ring because he couldn't have you any other way. He'll be up to his old tricks soon; mark my words." The vision of the dream woman turning to a tall, familiar dark-haired man and wrapping her lean body against his, made Sara clench her eyes shut. Dreams were supposed to fade once you woke, but this one had her in its clutches and would not let go.

She crawled out from under Jack's arm and the tangle of sheets and sat on the edge of the bed, letting the ocean air rustling through the sheer window coverings cool her overheated skin. The moonlight caught the diamond she wore, making her wince when it hit her square in the eye with its brilliance. Swallowing hard, she padded over to the enormous bathroom, shut the door and slid to the floor, letting tears roll down her face. Evidence of the intense session they'd shared last night lay all around her: Soft leather restraints, a bottle of expensive champagne, a vibrator and a bottle of lubricant. She squirmed on the floor, sore in places she didn't know she had.

Jack certainly knew how to throw a party. She brushed the tears away berating herself.

You liked it. Don't be such a hypocrite. You love giving him control over you this way.

The fact that he'd whisked her away on a surprise New Year's Eve junket to St. Bart's, to this remote, secluded and ultra-exclusive resort that "supported" their lifestyle choice had shocked the shit out of her at first. But by the time he'd worked her into a frenzy on the private jet and they'd emerged in the paradise of seventy-degree weather, ocean breezes and more of his fingers, lips, tongue and cock, she gave into it, loving every breathless minute.

"Hey," a soft knock and the sound of his deep, morning gravelly voice made her startle. "What's up in there?"

She stood, splashed water on her face and opened the door, smile fixed on her face. He frowned and pulled her into his arms. She sighed, letting the mysterious way he calmed her by his sheer presence work its magic. It was so strange, amazingly erotic, highly charged, and seemingly perfect – but for the dreams.

"I have an idea," he spoke into her hair.

"Huh, if it involves my ass again, we'd better wait twenty four hours." She giggled at his groan, felt his cock stir against her and suppressed her own surge of horniness.

"Seriously, I may not sit for a week. Not that I'm complaining."

"I am serious." He stepped back, took her face between his hands. His deep blue gaze did its usual song and dance on her emotions. "Marry me."

"I already said yes to that remember?" She flashed the giant ring she still couldn't adjust to on her finger. "Under duress I might add."

He smiled, ran a finger over her lips. "No. Today. Here."

About Liz Crowe

Microbrewery owner, best-selling author, beer blogger and journalist, mom of three teenagers, and soccer fan, Liz lives in the great Midwest, in a major college town. Years of experience in sales and fund raising, plus an eight-year stint as an ex-pat trailing spouse, plus making her way in a world of men (i.e. the beer industry), has prepped her for life as erotic romance author.

When she isn't sweating inventory and sales figures for the brewery, she can be found writing, editing or sweating promotional efforts for her latest publications.

Her groundbreaking romance subgenre, "Romance for Real Life," has gained thousands of fans and followers who are interested less in the "HEA" and more in the "WHA" ("What Happens After?")

Her beer blog **a2beerwench.com** is nationally recognized for its insider yet outsider views on the craft beer industry. Her books are set in the not-so-common worlds of breweries, on the soccer pitch and in high-powered real estate offices. Don't ask her for anything "like" a Budweiser or risk painful injury.

www.lizcrowe.com
www.brewingpasssion.com
www.a2beerwench.com
www.facebook.com/lizcroweauthor
www.twitter.com/beerwencha2
www.facebook.com/romanceforreallife
www.facebook.com/jackgordonrealtor
www.facebook.com/craigrobinsonmd

CPSIA information can be obtained at www.ICGtesting.com
Printed in the USA
LVOW05s1157050114

368155LV00015B/323/P